". . . if we can only have the help of other people, such as yourselves, on a worldwide scale, we can match our ancestors, or surpass them…not in their ways, which were often shortsighted and wasteful, but in achievements uniquely ours . . . ."

His voice trailed off. She wasn't listening. She stared over his head, into the air, and horror stood on her face.

Then trumpets howled on battlements, and the cathedral bells crashed to life.

"What the nine devils!" Ruori turned on his heel and looked up. The zenith had become quite blue. Lazily over S' Antón floated five orca shapes. The new sun glared off a jagged heraldry painted along their flanks. He estimated dizzily that each of them must be three hundred feet long.

Blood-colored things petaled out below them and drifted down upon the city.

"The Sky People!" said a small broken croak behind him. "Sant'sima Marí, pray for us now!"

Maurai & Kith

POUL ANDERSON

Maurai & Kith

TOR

A TOM DOHERTY ASSOCIATES BOOK

Copyright © 1982 by Poul Anderson

A TOR Book

First TOR printing, October 1982

ISBN: 48-545-X

Cover art by Thomas Kidd

Acknowledgements: The stories contained herein were first published and are copyright as follows:

"The Sky People": *The Magazine of Fantasy and Science Fiction,* copyright © 1959 by the Mercury Press, Inc.
"Progress": *The Magazine of Fantasy and Science Fiction,* copyright © 1962 by the Mercury Press, Inc.
"Windmill": *Saving Worlds,* copyright © 1973 by Roger Elwood.
"Ghetto": *The Magazine of Fantasy and Science Fiction,* copyright © 1953 by The Mercury Press, Inc.
"The Horn of Time the Hunter": *Amazing,* copyright © 1963 by Ultimate Publication, Inc.

Printed in the United States of America

Distributed by:
Pinnacle Books, Inc.
1430 Broadway
New York, New York 10018

CONTENTS

MAURAI

KITH

MAURAI

THE SKY PEOPLE

The rover fleet got there just before sunrise. From its height, five thousand feet, the land was bluish gray, smoked with mists. Irrigation canals caught the first light as if they were full of mercury. Westward the ocean gleamed, its far edge dissolved into purple and a few stars.

Loklann sunna Holber leaned over the gallery rail of his flagship and pointed a telescope at the city. It sprang to view as a huddle of walls, flat roofs, and square watchtowers. The cathedral spires were tinted rose by a hidden sun. No barrage balloons were aloft. It must be true what rumor said, that the Perio had abandoned its outlying provinces to their fate. So the portable wealth of Meyco would have flowed into S' Antón, for safekeeping—which meant that the place was well worth a raid. Loklann grinned.

Robra sunna Stam, the *Buffalo*'s mate, spoke. "Best we come down to about two thousand," he suggested. "To make sure the men aren't blown sideways, to the wrong side of the town walls."

"Aye." The skipper nodded his helmeted head. "Two thousand, so be it."

Their voices seemed oddly loud up here, where only the wind and a creak of rigging had broken silence. The sky around the rovers was dusky immensity, tinged red gold in the east. Dew lay on the gallery deck. But when the long wooden horns blew signals, it was somehow not an interruption, nor was the distant shouting of orders from other vessels, thud of crew feet, clatter of windlasses and hand-operated compressor pumps. To a Sky Man, those sounds belonged in the upper air.

Five great craft spiraled smoothly downward. The first sunrays flashed off gilt figureheads, bold on sharp gondola prows, and rioted along the extravagant designs painted on gas bags. Sails and rudders were unbelievably white across the last western darkness.

"Hullo, there," said Loklann. He had been studying the harbor through his telescope. "Something new. What could it be?"

He offered the tube to Robra, who held it to his remaining eye. Within the glass circle lay a stone dock and warehouses, centuries old, from the days of the Perio's greatness. Less than a fourth of their capacity was used now. The normal clutter of wretched little fishing craft, a single coasting schooner . . . and yes, by Oktai the Stormbringer, a monster thing, bigger than a whale, seven masts that were impossibly tall!

"I don't know." The mate lowered the telescope. "A foreigner? But where from? Nowhere in this continent—"

"I never saw any arrangement like that," said Loklann. "Square sails on the topmasts, fore-and-aft below." He stroked his short beard. It burned like spun copper in the morning light; he was one of the fair-haired blue-eyed men, rare even among the Sky People and unheard of elsewhere. "Of course," he said, "we're no experts on water craft. We only see them in passing." A not unamiable contempt rode his words: sailors made good slaves, at least, but naturally the only fit vehicle for a fighting man was a rover abroad and a horse at home.

"Probably a trader," he decided. "We'll capture it if possible."

He turned his attention to more urgent problems. He had no map of S' Antón, had never even seen it before. This was the farthest south any Sky People had yet gone plundering, and almost as far as any had ever visited; in bygone days aircraft were still too primitive and the Perio too strong. Thus Loklann must scan the city from far above, through drifting white vapors, and make his plan on the spot. Nor could it be very complicated, for he had only signal flags and a barrel-chested hollerer with a megaphone to pass orders to the other vessels.

"That big plaza in front of the temple," he murmured. "Our contingent will land there. Let the *Stormcloud* men tackle that big building east of it . . . see . . . it looks like a chief's dwelling. Over there, along the north wall, typical barracks and parade ground—*Coyote* can deal with the soldiers. Let the *Witch of Heaven* men land on the docks, seize the seaward gun emplacements and that strange vessel, then join the attack on the garrison. *Fire Elk*'s crew should land inside the east city gate and send a detachment to the south gate, to bottle in the civilian population. Having occupied the plaza, I'll send reinforcements wherever they're needed. All clear?''

He snapped down his goggles. Some of the big men crowding about him wore chain armor, but he preferred a cuirass of hardened leather, Mong style; it was nearly as strong and a lot lighter. He was armed with a pistol, but had more faith in his battle ax. An archer could shoot almost as fast as a gun, as accurately—and firearms were getting fabulously expensive to operate as sulfur sources dwindled.

He felt a tightness which was like being a little boy again, opening presents on Midwinter Morning. Oktai knew what treasures he would find, of gold, cloth, tools, slaves, of battle and high deeds and eternal fame. Possibly death. Someday he was sure to die in combat; he had sacrificed so much to his josses, they wouldn't grudge him war-death and a chance to be reborn as a Sky Man.

"Let's go!" he said.

He sprang up on a gallery rail and over. For a moment the world pinwheeled; now the city was on top and now again his *Buffalo* streaked past. Then he pulled the ripcord and his harness slammed him to steadiness. Around him, air bloomed with scarlet parachutes. He gauged the wind and tugged a line, guiding himself down.

Don Miwel Carabán, calde of S' Antón d' Inio, arranged a lavish feast for his Maurai guests. It was not only that this was a historic occasion, which might even mark a turning point in the long decline. (Don Miwel, being that rare combination, a practical man who could read, knew that the withdrawal of Perio troops to Brasil twenty years ago was not a "temporary adjustment." They would never come back. The outer provinces were on their own.) But the strangers must be convinced that they had found a nation rich, strong, and basically civilized, that it was worthwhile visiting the Meycan coasts to trade, ultimately to make alliance against the northern savages.

The banquet lasted till nearly midnight. Though some of the old irrigation canals had choked up and never been repaired, so that cactus and rattlesnake housed in abandoned pueblos, Meyco Province was still fertile. The slant-eyed Mong horsemen from Tekkas had killed off innumerable peons when they raided five years back; wooden pitchforks and obsidian hoes were small use against saber and arrow. It would be another decade before population had returned to normal and the periodic famines resumed. Thus Don Miwel offered many courses, beef, spiced ham, olives, fruits, wines, nuts, coffee, which last the Sea People were unfamiliar with and didn't much care for, et cetera. Entertainment followed—music, jugglers, a fencing exhibition by some of the young nobles.

At this point the surgeon of the *Dolphin*, who was rather drunk, offered to show an Island dance.

Muscular beneath tattoos, his brown form went through a series of contortions which pursed the lips of the dignified Dons. Miwel himself remarked, "It reminds me somewhat of our peons' fertility rites," with a strained courtesy that suggested to Captain Ruori Rangi Lohannaso that peons had an altogether different and not very nice culture.

The surgeon threw back his queue and grinned. "Now let's bring the ship's wahines ashore to give them a real hula," he said in Maurai-Ingliss.

"No," answered Ruori. "I fear we may have shocked them already. The proverb goes, 'When in the Solmon Islands, darken your skin.'"

"I don't think they know how to have any fun," complained the doctor.

"We don't yet know what the taboos are," warned Ruori. "Let us be as grave, then, as these spike-bearded men, and not laugh or make love until we are back on shipboard among our wahines."

"But it's stupid! Shark-toothed Nan eat me if I'm going to—"

"Your ancestors are ashamed," said Ruori. It was about as sharp a rebuke as you could give a man whom you didn't intend to fight. He softened his tone to take out the worst sting, but the doctor had to shut up. Which he did, mumbling an apology and retiring with his blushes to a dark corner beneath faded murals.

Ruori turned back to his host. "I beg your pardon, S'ñor," he said, using the local tongue. "My men's command of Spañol is even less than my own."

"Of course." Don Miwel's lean black-clad form made a stiff little bow. It brought his sword up, ludicrously, like a tail. Ruori heard a smothered snort of laughter from among his officers. And yet, thought the captain, were long trousers and ruffled shirt any worse than sarong, sandals, and clan tattoos? Different customs, no more. You had to sail the Maurai Federation, from Awaii to his own N'Zealann and west to Mlaya, before you appreciated how big this planet was and how much of it a mystery.

"You speak our language most excellently, S'ñor," said Doñita Tresa Carabán. She smiled. "Perhaps better than we, since you studied texts centuries old before embarking, and the Spañol has changed greatly since."

Ruori smiled back. Don Miwel's daughter was worth it. The rich black dress caressed a figure as good as any in the world; and, while the Sea People paid less attention to a woman's face, he saw that hers was proud and well formed, her father's eagle beak softened to a curve, luminous eyes and hair the color of midnight oceans. It was too bad these Meycans—the nobles, at least—thought a girl should be reserved solely for the husband they eventually picked for her. He would have liked her to swap her pearls and silver for a lei and go out in a ship's canoe, just the two of them, to watch the sunrise and make love.

However—

"In such company," he murmured, "I am stimulated to learn the modern language as fast as possible."

She refrained from coquetting with her fan, a local habit the Sea People found alternately hilarious and irritating. But her lashes fluttered. They were very long, and her eyes, he saw, were gold-flecked green.

"You are learning cab'llero manners just as fast, S'ñor," she said.

"Do not call our language 'modern,' I pray you," interrupted a scholarly-looking man in a long robe. Ruori recognized Bispo Don Carlos Ermosillo, a high priest of that Esu Carito who seemed cognate with the Maurai Lesu Haristi. "Not modern, but corrupt. I too have studied ancient books, printed before the War of Judgment. Our ancestors spoke the true Spañol. Our version of it is as distorted as our present-day society." He sighed. "But what can one expect, when even among the well born, not one in ten can write his own name?"

"There was more literacy in the high days of the Perio," said Don Miwel. "You should have visited us a hundred years ago, S'ñor Captain, and seen what our race was capable of."

"Yet what was the Perio itself but a successor state?" asked the Bispo bitterly. "It unified a large area, gave law and order for a while, but what did it create that was new? Its course was the same sorry tale as a thousand kingdoms before, and therefore the same judgment has fallen on it."

Doñita Tresa crossed herself. Even Ruori, who held a degree in engineering as well as navigation, was shocked. "Not atomics?" he exclaimed.

"What? Oh. The old weapons, which destroyed the old world. No, of course not." Don Carlos shook his head. "But in our more limited way, we have been as stupid and sinful as the legendary forefathers, and the results have been parallel. You may call it human greed or el Dío's punishment as you will; I think the two mean much the same thing."

Ruori looked closely at the priest. "I should like to speak with you further, S'ñor," he said, hoping it was the right title. "Men who know history, rather than myth, are rare these days."

"By all means," said Don Carlos. "I should be honored."

Doñita Tresa shifted on light, impatient feet. "It is customary to dance," she said.

Her father laughed. "Ah, yes. The young ladies have been getting quite impatient, I am sure. Time enough to resume formal discussions tomorrow, S'ñor Captain. Now let the music begin."

He signalled. The orchestra struck up. Some instruments were quite like those of the Maurai, others wholly unfamiliar. The scale itself was different . . . They had something like it in Stralia, but —a hand fell on Ruori's arm. He looked down at Tresa. "Since you do not ask me to dance," she said, "may I be so immodest as to ask you?"

"What does 'immodest' mean?" he inquired.

She blushed and tried to explain, without success. Ruori decided it was another local concept which the Sea People lacked. By that time the Meycan girls and their cavaliers were out on the ballroom floor. He studied them for a moment. "The motions are unknown to me," he said, "but I think I could soon learn."

She slipped into his arms. It was a pleasant contact, even though nothing would come of it. "You do very well," she said after a minute. "Are all your folk so graceful?"

Only later did he realize that was a compliment for which he should have thanked her; being an

Islander, he took it at face value as a question and replied, "Most of us spend a great deal of time on the water. A sense of balance and rhythm must be developed or one is likely to fall into the sea."

She wrinkled her nose. "Oh, stop," she laughed. "You're as solemn as S' Osé in the cathedral."

Ruori grinned back. He was a tall young man, brown as all his race but with the gray eyes which many bore in memory of Ingliss ancestors. Being a N'Zealanner, he was not tattooed as lavishly as some Federation men. On the other hand, he had woven a whalebone filigree into his queue, his sarong was the finest batik, and he had added thereto a fringed shirt. His knife, without which a Maurai felt obscenely helpless, was in contrast: old, shabby until you saw the blade, a tool.

"I must see this god, S' Osé," he said. "Will you show me? Or no, I would not have eyes for a mere statue."

"How long will you stay?" she asked.

"As long as we can. We are supposed to explore the whole Meycan coast. Hitherto the only Maurai contact with the Merikan continent has been one voyage from Awaii to Calforni. They found desert and a few savages. We have heard from Okkaidan traders that there are forests still farther north, where yellow and white men strive against each other. But what lies south of Calforni was unknown to us until this expedition was sent out. Perhaps you can tell us what to expect in Su-Merika."

"Little enough by now," she sighed, "even in Brasil."

"Ah, but lovely roses bloom in Meyco."

Her humor returned. "And flattering words in N'Zealann," she chuckled.

"Far from it. We are notoriously straightforward. Except, of course, when yarning about voyages we have made."

"What yarns will you tell about this one?"

"Not many, lest all the young men of the Federation come crowding here. But I will take you aboard my ship, Doñita, and show you to the compass. Thereafter it will always point toward S' Antón d' Inio. You will be, so to speak, my compass rose."

Somewhat to his surprise, she understood, and laughed. She led him across the floor, supple between his hands.

Thereafter, as the night wore on, they danced together as much as decency allowed, or a bit more, and various foolishness which concerned no one else passed between them. Toward sunrise the orchestra was dismissed and the guests, hiding yawns behind well-bred hands, began to take their departure.

"How dreary to stand and receive farewells," whispered Tresa. "Let them think I went to bed already." She took Ruori's hand and slipped behind a column and thence out onto a balcony. An aged serving woman, stationed to act as duenna for couples that wandered thither, had wrapped up in her mantle against the cold and fallen asleep. Otherwise the two were alone among jasmines. Mists floated around the palace and blurred the city; far off rang the *"Todos buen"* of pikemen tramping the outer walls. Westward the balcony faced darkness, where the last stars glittered. The seven tall topmasts of the Maurai *Dolphin* caught the earliest sun and glowed.

Tresa shivered and stood close to Ruori. They did not speak for a while.

"Remember us," she said at last, very low. "When you are back with your own happier people, do not forget us here."

"How could I?" he answered, no longer in jest.

"You have so much more than we," she said wistfully. "You have told me how your ships can sail unbelievably fast, almost into the wind. How your fishers always fill their nets, how your whale ranchers keep herds that darken the water, how you even farm the ocean for food and fiber and . . ." She fingered the shimmering material of his shirt. "You told me this was made by craft out of fishbones. You told me that every family has its own spacious house and every member of it, almost, his own boat . . . that even small children on the loneliest island can read, and have printed books . . . that you have none of the sicknesses which destroy us . . . that no one hungers and all are free—oh, do not forget us, you on whom el Dío has smiled!"

She stopped, then, embarrassed. He could see how her head lifted and nostrils dilated, as if resenting him. After all, he thought, she came from a breed which for centuries had given, not received, charity.

Therefore he chose his words with care. "It has been less our virtue than our good fortune, Doñita. We suffered less than most in the War of Judgment, and our being chiefly Islanders prevented our population from outrunning the sea's rich ability to feed us. So we—no, we did not retain any lost ancestral arts. There are none. But we did re-create an ancient attitude, a way of thinking, which has made the difference—science."

She crossed herself. "The atom!" she breathed, drawing from him.

"No, no, Doñita," he protested. "So many nations we have discovered lately believe science was the cause of the old world's ruin. Or else they think it was a collection of cut-and-dried formulas for making tall buildings or talking at a distance. But neither is true. The scientific method is only a means of learning. It is a . . . a perpetual starting afresh. And that is why you people here in Meyco can help us as much as we can help you, why we have sought you out and will come knocking hopefully at your doors again in the future."

She frowned, though something began to glow within her. "I do not understand," she said.

He cast about for an example. At last he pointed to a series of small holes in the balcony rail. "What used to be here?" he asked.

"Why . . . I do not know. It has always been like that."

"I think I can tell you. I have seen similar things elsewhere. It was a wrought-iron grille. But it was pulled out a long time ago and made into weapons or tools. No?"

"Quite likely," she admitted. "Iron and copper have grown very scarce. We have to send caravans across the whole land, to Támico ruins, in great peril from bandits and barbarians, to fetch our metal. Time was when there were iron rails within a kilometer of this place. Don Carlos has told me."

He nodded. "Just so. The ancients exhausted the world. They mined the ores, burned the oil and coal, eroded the land, until nothing was left. I exaggerate, of course. There are still deposits. But not enough.

The old civilization used up the capital, so to speak. Now sufficient forest and soil have come back that the world would try to reconstruct machine culture— except that there aren't enough minerals and fuels. For centuries men have been forced to tear up the antique artifacts, if they were to have any metal at all. By and large, the knowledge of the ancients hasn't been lost; it has simply become unusable, because we are so much poorer than they."

He leaned forward, earnestly. "But knowledge and discovery do not depend on wealth," he said. "Perhaps because we did not have much metal to cannibalize in the Islands, we turned elsewhere. The scientific method is just as applicable to wind and sun and living matter as it was to oil, iron, or uranium. By studying genetics we learned how to create sea-weeds, plankton, fish that would serve our purposes. Scientific forest management gives us adequate timber, organic-synthesis bases, some fuel. The sun pours down energy which we know how to concentrate and use. Wood, ceramics, even stone can replace metal for most purposes. The wind, through such principles as the airfoil or the Venturi law or the Hilsch tube, supplies force, heat, refrigeration; the tides can be harnessed. Even in its present early stage, paramathematical psychology helps control population, as well as—no, I am talking like an engineer now, falling into my own language. I apologize.

"What I wanted to say was that if we can only have the help of other people, such as yourselves, on a worldwide scale, we can match our ancestors, or surpass them . . . not in their ways, which were often shortsighted and wasteful, but in achievements uniquely ours . . . ."

His voice trailed off. She wasn't listening. She stared over his head, into the air, and horror stood on her face.

Then trumpets howled on battlements, and the cathedral bells crashed to life.

"What the nine devils!" Ruori turned on his heel and looked up. The zenith had become quite blue. Lazily over S' Antón floated five orca shapes. The new sun glared off a jagged heraldry painted along their flanks. He estimated dizzily that each of them must be three hundred feet long.

Blood-colored things petaled out below them and drifted down upon the city.

"The Sky People!" said a small broken croak behind him. "Sant'sima Marí, pray for us now!"

Loklann hit flagstones, rolled over, and bounced to his feet. Beside him a carved horseman presided over fountain waters. For an instant he admired the stone, almost alive; they had nothing like that in Canyon, Zona, Corado, any of the mountain kingdoms. And the temple facing this plaza was white skywardness.

The square had been busy, farmers and handi-crafters setting up their booths for a market day. Most of them scattered in noisy panic. But one big man roared, snatched a stone hammer, and dashed in his rags to meet Loklann. He was covering the flight of a young woman, probably his wife, who held a baby in her arms. Through the shapeless sack dress Loklann saw that her figure wasn't bad. She would fetch a price when the Mong slave dealer next visited Canyon. So could her husband, but there wasn't time now, still encumbered with a chute. Loklann whipped out his pistol and fired. The man fell to his knees, gaped at the blood seeping between fingers clutched to his belly, and collapsed. Loklann flung off his harness. His boots thudded after the woman. She shrieked when fingers closed on her arm and tried to wriggle free, but the brat hampered her. Loklann shoved her toward the temple. Robra was already on its steps.

"Post a guard!" yelled the skipper. "We may as well keep prisoners in here, till we're ready to plunder it."

An old man in priest's robes tottered to the door. He held up one of the cross-shaped Meycan josses, as if to bar the way. Robra brained him with an ax blow, kicked the body off the stairs, and urged the woman inside.

It sleeted armed men. Locklann winded his oxhorn bugle, rallying them. A counterattack could be expected any minute . . . . Yes, now.

A troop of Meycan cavalry clanged into view. They were young, proud-looking men in baggy pants, leather breastplate and plumed helmet, blowing cloak, fire-hardened wooden lances but steel sabres— very much like the yellow nomads of Tekkas, whom they had fought for centuries. But so had the Sky People. Loklann pounded to the head of his line, where his standard bearer had raised the Lightning Flag. Half the *Buffalo*'s crew fitted together sections of pike tipped with edged ceramic, grounded the butts, and waited. The charge crested upon them. Their pikes slanted down. Some horses spitted themselves, others reared back screaming. The pikemen jabbed at their riders. The second paratroop line stepped in, ax and sword and hamstringing knife. For a few minutes murder boiled. The Meycans broke. They did not flee, but they retreated in confusion. And then the Canyon bows began to snap.

Presently only dead and hurt cluttered the square. Loklann moved briskly among the latter. Those who weren't too badly wounded were hustled into the temple. Might as well collect all possible slaves and cull them later.

From afar he heard a dull boom. "Cannon," said Robra, joining him. "At the army barracks."

"Well, let the artillery have its fun, till our boys get in among 'em," said Loklann sardonically.

"Sure, sure." Robra looked nervous. "I wish they'd let us hear from them, though. Just standing around here isn't good."

"It won't be long," predicted Loklann.

Nor was it. A runner with a broken arm staggered to him. *"Stormcloud,"* he gasped. "The big building you sent us against . . . full of swordsmen . . . . They repulsed us at the door—"

"Huh! I thought it was only the king's house," said Loklann. He laughed. "Well, maybe the king was giving a party. Come on, then, I'll go see for myself. Robra, take over here." His finger swept out thirty men to accompany him. They jogged down streets empty and silent except for their bootfalls and weapon-jingle. The housefolk must be huddled terrified behind those blank walls. So much the easier to corral them later, when the fighting was done and the looting began.

A roar broke loose. Loklann led a dash around a

last corner. Opposite him he saw the palace, an old building, red-tiled roof and mellow walls and many glass windows. The *Stormcloud* men were fighting at the main door. Their dead and wounded from the last attack lay thick.

Loklann took in the situation at a glance. "It wouldn't occur to those lardheads to send a detachment through some side entrance, would it?" he groaned. "Jonak, take fifteen of our boys and batter in a lesser door and hit the rear of that line. The rest of you help me keep it busy meanwhile."

He raised his red-spattered ax. "A Canyon!" he yelled. "A Canyon!" His followers bellowed behind him and they ran to battle.

The last charge had reeled away bloody and breathless. Half a dozen Meycans stood in the wide doorway. They were nobles: grim men with goatees and waxed mustaches, in formal black, red cloaks wrapped as shields on their left arms and long slim swords in their right hands. Behind them stood others, ready to take the place of the fallen.

"A Canyon!" shouted Loklann as he rushed.

"*Quel Dío wela!*" cried a tall grizzled Don. A gold chain of office hung around his neck. His blade snaked forth.

Loklann flung up his ax and parried. The Don was fast, riposting with a lunge that ended on the raider's breast. But hardened six-ply leather turned the point. Loklann's men crowded on either side, reckless of thrusts, and hewed. He struck the enemy sword; it spun from the owner's grasp. "*Ah, no, Don Miwel!*" cried a young person beside the calde. The older man snarled, threw out his hands, and somehow clamped them on Loklann's ax. He yanked it away with a troll's strength. Loklann stared into eyes that said death. Don Miwel raised the ax. Loklann drew his pistol and fired point blank.

As Don Miwel toppled, Loklann caught him, pulled off the gold chain, and threw it around his own neck. Straightening, he met a savage thrust. It glanced off his helmet. He got his ax back, planted his feet firmly, and smote.

The defending line buckled.

Clamor lifted behind Loklann. He turned and saw weapons gleam beyond his own men's shoulders. With a curse he realized—there had been more people in the palace than these holding the main door. The rest had sallied out the rear and were now on his back!

A point pierced his thigh. He felt no more than a sting, but rage flapped black before his eyes. "Be reborn as the swine you are!" he roared. Half unaware, he thundered loose, cleared a space for himself, lurched aside and oversaw the battle.

The newcomers were mostly palace guards, judging from their gaily striped uniforms, pikes, and machetes. But they had allies, a dozen men such as Loklann had never seen or heard of. Those had the brown skin and black hair of Injuns, but their faces were more like a white man's; intricate blue designs covered their bodies, which were clad only in wraparounds and flower wreaths. They wielded knives and clubs with wicked skill.

Loklann tore his trouser leg open to look at his wound. It wasn't much. More serious was the beating his men were taking. He saw Mork sunna Brenn rush,

sword uplifted, at one of the dark strangers, a big
man who had added a rich-looking blouse to his skirt.
Mork had killed four men at home for certain, in law-
ful fights, and nobody knew how many abroad. The
dark man waited, a knife between his teeth, hands
hanging loose. As the blade came down, the dark
man simply wasn't there. Grinning around his knife,
he chopped at the sword wrist with the edge of a
hand. Loklann distinctly heard bones crack. Mork
yelled. The foreigner hit him in the Adam's apple.
Mork went to his knees, spat blood, caved in, and was
still. Another Sky Man charged, ax aloft. The stranger
again evaded the weapon, caught the moving body
on his hip, and helped it along. The Sky Man hit the
pavement with his head and moved no more.

Now Loklann saw that the newcomers were a ring
around others who did not fight. Women. By Oktai
and man-eating Ulagu, these bastards were leading
out all the women in the palace! And the fighting
against them had broken up; surly raiders stood back
nursing their wounds.

Loklann ran forward. "A Canyon! A Canyon!" he
shouted.

"Ruori Rangi Lohannaso," said the big stranger
politely. He rapped a string of orders. His party
began to move away.

"Hit them, you scum!" bawled Loklann. His men
rallied and straggled after. Rearguard pikes prodded
them back. Loklann led a rush to the front of the
hollow square.

The big man saw him coming. Gray eyes focused
on the calde's chain and became full winter. "So you
killed Don Miwel," said Ruori in Spañol. Loklann

understood him, having learned the tongue from prisoners and concubines during many raids further north. "You lousy son of a skua."

Loklann's pistol rose. Ruori's hand blurred. Suddenly the knife stood in the Sky Man's right biceps. He dropped his gun. "I'll want that back!" shouted Ruori. Then, to his followers: "Come, to the ship."

Loklann stared at blood rivering down his arm. He heard a clatter as the refugees broke through the weary Canyon line. Jonak's party appeared in the main door—which was now empty, its surviving defenders having left with Ruori.

A man approached Loklann, who still regarded his arm. "Shall we go after 'em, Skipper?" he said, almost timidly. "Jonak can lead us after 'em."

"No," said Loklann.

"But they must be escorting a hundred women. A lot of young women too."

Loklann shook himself, like a dog coming out of a deep cold stream. "No. I want to find the medic and get this wound stitched. Then we'll have a lot else to do. We can settle with those outlanders later, if the chance comes. Man, we've a city to sack!"

There were dead men scattered on the wharves, some burned. They looked oddly small beneath the warehouses, like rag dolls tossed away by a weeping child. Cannon fumes lingered to bite nostrils.

Atel Hamid Seraio, the mate, who had been left aboard the *Dolphin* with the enlisted crew, led a band to meet Ruori. His salute was in the Island manner, so casual that even at this moment several of the Meycans looked shocked. "We were about to come for you, Captain," he said.

Ruori looked toward that forest which was the *Dolphin*'s rig. "What happened here?" he asked.

"A band of those devils landed near the battery. They took the emplacements while we were still wondering what it was all about. Part of them went off toward that racket in the north quarter, I believe where the army lives. But the rest of the gang attacked us. Well, with our gunwale ten feet above the dock, and us trained to repel pirates, they didn't have much luck. I gave them a dose of flame."

Ruori winced from the blackened corpses. Doubtless they had deserved it, but he didn't like the idea of pumping flaming blubber oil across live men.

"Too bad they didn't try from the seaward side," added Atel with a sigh. "We've got such a lovely harpoon catapult. I used one like it years ago off Hinja, when a Sinese buccaneer came too close. His junk sounded like a whale."

"Men aren't whales!" snapped Ruori.

"All right, Captain, all right, all right." Atel backed away from his violence, a little frightened. "No ill-speaking meant."

Ruori recollected himself and folded his hands. "I spoke in needless anger," he said formally. "I laugh at myself."

"It's nothing, Captain. As I was saying, we beat them off and they finally withdrew. I imagine they'll bring back reinforcements. What shall we do?"

"That's what I don't know," said Ruori in a bleak tone. He turned to the Meycans, who stood with stricken, uncomprehending faces. "Your pardon is prayed, Dons and Doñitas," he said in Spañol. "He was only relating to me what had happened."

"Don't apologize!" Tresa Carabán spoke, stepping out ahead of the men. Some of them looked a bit offended, but they were too tired and stunned to reprove her forwardness, and to Ruori it was only natural that a woman act as freely as a man. "You saved our lives, Captain. More than our lives."

He wondered what was worse than death, then nodded. Slavery, of course—ropes and whips and a lifetime's unfree toil in a strange land. His eyes dwelt upon her, the long hair disheveled past smooth shoulders, gown ripped, weariness and a streak of tears across her face. He wondered if she knew her father was dead. She held herself straight and regarded him with an odd defiance.

"We are uncertain what to do," he said awkwardly. "We are only fifty men. Can we help your city?"

A young nobleman, swaying on his feet, replied: "No. The city is done. You can take these ladies to safety, that is all."

Tresa protested: "You are not surrendering already, S'ñor Dónoju!"

"No, Doñita," the young man breathed. "But I hope I can be shriven before returning to fight, for I am a dead man."

"Come aboard," said Ruori curtly.

He led the way up the gangplank. Liliu, one of the ship's five wahines, ran to meet him. She threw arms about his neck and cried, "I feared you were slain!"

"Not yet." Ruori disengaged her as gently as

possible. He noticed Tresa standing stiff, glaring at them both. Puzzlement came—did these curious Meycans expect a crew to embark on a voyage of months without taking a few girls along? Then he decided that the wahines' clothing, being much like his men's, was against local mores. To Nan with their silly prejudices. But it hurt that Tresa drew away from him.

The other Meycans stared about them. Not all had toured the ship when she first arrived. They looked in bewilderment at lines and spans, down fathoms of deck to the harpoon catapult, capstans, bowsprit, and back at the sailors. The Maurai grinned encouragingly. Thus far most of them looked on this as a lark. Men who skindove after sharks, for fun, or who sailed outrigger canoes alone across a thousand ocean miles to pay a visit, were not put out by a fight.

But they had not talked with grave Don Miwel and merry Don Wan and gentle Bispo Ermosillo, and then seen those people dead on a dance floor, thought Ruori in bitterness.

The Meycan women huddled together, ladies and servants, to weep among each other. The palace guards formed a solid rank around them. The nobles, and Tresa, followed Ruori up on the poop deck.

"Now," he said, "let us talk. Who are these bandits?"

"The Sky People," whispered Tresa.

"I can see that." Ruori cocked an eye on the aircraft patrolling overhead. They had the sinister beauty of as many barracuda. Here and there columns of smoke reached toward them. "But who are they? Where from?"

"They are Nor-Merikans," she answered in a dry little voice, as if afraid to give it color. "From the wild highlands around the Corado River, the Grand Canyon it has cut for itself—mountaineers. There is a story that they were driven from the eastern plains by Mong invaders, a long time ago; but as they grew strong in the hills and deserts, they defeated some Mong tribes and became friendly with others. For a hundred years they have harried our northern borders. This is the first time they have ventured so far south. We never expected them—I suppose their spies learned most of our soldiers are along the Río Gran, chasing a rebel force. They sailed south-westerly, above our land—" She shivered.

The young Dónoju spat. "They are heathen dogs! They know nothing but to rob and burn and kill!" He sagged. "What have we done that they are loosed on us?"

Ruori rubbed his chin thoughtfully. "They can't be quite such savages," he murmured. "Those blimps are better than anything my own Federation has tried to make. The fabric . . . some tricky synthetic? It must be, or it wouldn't contain hydrogen any length of time. Surely they don't use helium! But for hydrogen production on that scale, you need industry. A good empirical chemistry, at least. They might even electrolyze it . . . good Lesu!"

He realized he had been talking to himself in his home language. "I beg your pardon," he said. "I was wondering what we might do. This ship carries no flying vessels."

Again he looked upward. Atel handed him his binoculars. He focused on the nearest blimp. The huge gas bag and the gondola beneath—itself as big as many a Maurai ship—formed an aerodynamically clean unit. The gondola seemed to be light, woven cane about a wooden frame, but strong. Three-fourths of the way up from its keel a sort of gallery ran clear around, on which the crew might walk and work. At intervals along the rail stood muscle-powered machines. Some must be for hauling, but others suggested catapults. Evidently the blimps of various chiefs fought each other occasionally, in the northern kingdoms. That might be worth knowing. The Federation's political psychologists were skilled at the divide-and-rule game. But for now . . .

The motive power was extraordinarily interesting. Near the gondola bows two lateral spars reached out for some fifty feet, one above the other. They supported two pivoted frames on either side, to which square sails were bent. A similar pair of spars pierced the after hull: eight sails in all. A couple of small retractable windwheels, vaned and pivoted, jutted beneath the gondola, evidently serving the purpose of a false keel. Sails and rudders were trimmed by lines running through block and tackle to windlasses on the gallery. By altering their set, it should be possible to steer at least several points to windward. And, yes, the air moves in different directions at different levels. A blimp could descend by pumping out cells in its gas bag, compressing the hydrogen into storage tanks; it could rise by reinflating or by dropping ballast (though the latter trick would be reserved for home stretches, when leakage had depleted the gas supply). Between sails, rudders, and its ability to find a reasonably favoring wind, such a blimp could go roving across several thousand miles, with a payload of several tons. Oh, a lovely craft!

Ruori lowered his glasses. "Hasn't the Perio built any air vessels, to fight back?" he asked.

"No," mumbled one of the Meycans. "All we ever had was balloons. We don't know how to make a fabric which will hold the lifting-gas long enough, or how to control the flight . . . ." His voice trailed off.

"And being a nonscientific culture, you never thought of doing systematic research to learn those tricks," said Ruori.

Tresa, who had been staring at her city, whirled about upon him. "It's easy for you!" she screamed. "You haven't stood off Mong in the north and Raucanians in the south for century after century. You haven't had to spend twenty years and ten thousand lives making canals and aqueducts, so a few less people would starve. You aren't burdened with a peon majority who can only work, who cannot look after themselves because they have never been taught how because their existence is too much of a burden for our land to afford it. It's easy for you to float about with your shirtless doxies and poke fun at us! What would you have done, S'ñor Almighty Captain?"

"Be still," reproved young Dónoju. "He saved our lives."

"So far!" she said, through teeth and tears. One small dancing shoe stamped the deck.

For a bemused moment, irrelevantly, Ruori wondered what a doxie was. It sounded uncomplimentary. Could she mean the wahines? But was there a more honorable way for a woman to earn a good dowry than by hazarding her life, side by side with the men of her people, on a mission of discovery and civilization? What did Tresa expect to tell her grandchildren about on rainy nights?

Then he wondered further why she should disturb him. He had noticed it before, in some of the Meycans, an almost terrifying intensity between man and wife, as if a spouse were somehow more than a respected friend and partner. But what other relationship was possible? A psychological specialist might know; Ruori was lost.

He shook an angry head, to clear it, and said aloud: "This is no time for inurbanity." He had to use a Spañol word with not quite the same connotation. "We must decide. Are you certain we have no hope of repelling the pirates?"

"Not unless S' Antón himself passes a miracle," said Doñoju in a dead voice.

Then, snapping erect: "There is only a single thing you can do for us, S'ñor. If you will leave now, with the women—there are high-born ladies among them, who must not be sold into captivity and disgrace. Bear them south to Port Wanawato, where the calde will look after their welfare."

"I do not like to run off," said Ruori, looking at the men fallen on the wharf.

"S'ñor, these are *ladies!* In el Dío's name, have mercy on them!"

Ruori studied the taut, bearded faces. He did owe them a great deal of hospitality, and he could see no other way he might ever repay it. "If you wish," he said slowly. "What of yourselves?"

The young noble bowed as if to a king. "Our

thanks and prayers will go with you, my lord Captain. We men, of course, will now return to battle." He stood up and barked in a parade-ground voice: "Atten-tion! Form ranks!"

A few swift kisses passed on the main deck, and then the men of Meyco had crossed the gangplank and tramped into their city.

Ruori beat a fist on the taffrail. "If we had some way," he mumbled. "If I could do something." Almost hopefully: "Do you think the bandits might attack us?"

"Only if you remain here," said Tresa. Her eyes were chips of green ice. "Would to Marí you had not pledged yourself to sail!"

"If they come after us at sea—"

"I do not think they will. You carry a hundred women and a few trade goods. The Sky People will have their pick of ten thousand women, as many men, and our city's treasures. Why should they take the trouble to pursue you?"

"Aye . . . aye . . . ."

"Go," she said. "You dare not linger."

Her coldness was like a blow. "What do you mean?" he asked. "Do you think the Maurai are cowards?"

She hesitated. Then, in reluctant honesty: "No."

"Well, why do you scoff at me?"

"Oh, go away!" She knelt by the rail, bowed head in arms, and surrendered to herself.

Ruori left her and gave his orders. Men scrambled into the rigging. Furled canvas broke loose and cracked in a young wind. Beyond the jetty, the ocean glittered blue, with small whitecaps; gulls skimmed across heaven. Ruori saw only the glimpses he had had before, as he led the retreat from the palace.

A weaponless man, his head split open. A girl, hardly twelve years old, who screamed as two raiders carried her into an alley. An aged man fleeing in terror, zigzagging, while four archers took potshots at him and howled laughter when he fell transfixed and dragged himself along on his hands. A woman sitting dumb in the street, her dress torn, next to a baby whose brains had been dashed out. A little statue in a niche, a holy image, a faded bunch of violets at its feet, beheaded by a casual war-hammer. A house that burned, and shrieks from within.

Suddenly the aircraft overhead were not beautiful. To reach up and pull them out of the sky!

Ruori stopped dead. The crew surged around him. He heard a short-haul chantey, deep voices vigorous from always having been free and well fed, but it echoed in a far corner of his brain.

"Casting off," sang the mate.

"Not yet! Not yet! Wait!"

Ruori ran toward the poop, up the ladder and past the steersman to Doñita Tresa. She had risen again, to stand with bent head past which the hair swept to hide her countenance.

"Tresa," panted Ruori. "Tresa, I've an idea. I think—there may be a chance—perhaps we can fight back after all."

She raised her eyes. Her fingers closed on his arm till he felt the nails draw blood.

Words tumbled from him. "It will depend . . . on luring them . . . to us. At least a couple of their vessels . . . must follow us . . . to sea. I think then

—I'm not sure of the details, but it may be . . . we can fight . . . even drive them off—"

Still she stared at him. He felt a hesitation. "Of course," he said, "we may lose the fight. And we do have the women aboard."

"If you lose," she asked, so low he could scarcely hear it, "will we die or be captured?"

"I think we will die."

"That is well." She nodded. "Yes. Fight, then."

"There is one thing I am unsure of. How to make them pursue us." He paused. "If someone were to let himself . . . be captured by them—and told them we were carrying off a great treasure—would they believe that?"

"They might well." Life had come back to her tones, even eagerness. "Let us say, the calde's hoard. None ever existed, but the robbers would believe my father's cellars were stuffed with gold."

"Then someone must go to them." Ruori turned his back to her, twisted his fingers together and slogged toward a conclusion he did not want to reach. "But it could not be just anyone. They would club a man in among the other slaves, would they not? I mean, would they listen to him at all?"

"Probably not. Very few of them know Spañol. By the time a man who babbled of treasure was understood, they might be halfway home." Tresa scowled. "What shall we do?"

Ruori saw the answer, but could not get it past his throat.

"I am sorry," he mumbled. "My idea was not so good after all. Let us be gone."

The girl forced her way between him and the rail to

stand in front of him, touching as if they danced again. Her voice was altogether steady. "You know a way."

"I do not."

"I have come to know you well, in one night. You are a poor liar. Tell me."

He looked away. Somehow, he got out: "A woman —not any woman, but a very beautiful one—would she not soon be taken to their chief?"

Tresa stood aside. The color drained from her cheeks.

"Yes," she said at last. "I think so."

"But then again," said Ruori wretchedly, "she might be killed. They do much wanton killing, those men. I cannot let anyone who was given into my protection risk death."

"You heathen fool," she said through tight lips. "Do you think the chance of being killed matters to me?"

"What else could happen?" he asked, surprised. And then: "Oh, yes, of course, the woman would be a slave if we lost the battle afterward. Though I should imagine, if she is beautiful, she would not be badly treated."

"And is that all you—" Tresa stopped. He had never known it was possible for a smile to show pure hurt. "Of course. I should have realized. Your people have your own ways of thinking."

"What do you mean?" he fumbled.

A moment more she stood with clenched fists. Then, half to herself: "They killed my father; yes, I saw him dead in the doorway. They would leave my city a ruin peopled by corpses."

Her head lifted. "I will go," she said.

"You?" He grabbed her shoulders. "No, surely not you! One of the others—"

"Should I send anybody else? I am the calde's daughter."

She pulled herself free of him and hurried across the deck, down the ladder toward the gangway. Her gaze was turned from the ship. A few words drifted back. "Afterward, if there is an afterward, there is always the convent."

He did not understand. He stood on the poop, staring after her and abominating himself until she was lost to sight. Then he said, "Cast off," and the ship stood out to sea.

The Meycans fought doggedly, street by street and house by house, but in a couple of hours their surviving soldiers had been driven into the northeast corner of S' Antón. They themselves hardly knew that, but a Sky chief had a view from above; a rover was now tethered to the cathedral, with a rope ladder for men to go up and down, and the companion vessel, skeleton crewed, brought their news to it.

"Good enough," said Loklann. "We'll keep them boxed in with a quarter of our force. I don't think they'll sally. Meanwhile the rest of us can get things organized. Let's not give these creatures too much time to hide themselves and their silver. In the afternoon, when we're rested, we can land parachuters behind the city troops, drive them out into our lines and destroy them."

He ordered the *Buffalo* grounded, that he might load the most precious loot at once. The men, by and large, were too rough—good lads, but apt to damage a robe or a cup or a jeweled cross in their haste; and sometimes those Meycan things were too beautiful even to give away, let alone sell.

The flagship descended as far as possible. It still hung at a thousand feet, for hand pumps and aluminum-alloy tanks did not allow much hydrogen compression. In colder, denser air it would have been suspended even higher. But ropes snaked from it to a quickly assembled ground crew. At home there were ratcheted capstans outside every lodge, enabling as few as four women to bring down a rover. One hated the emergency procedure of bleeding gas, for the Keepers could barely meet demand, in spite of a new sunpower unit added to their hydroelectric station, and charged accordingly. (Or so the Keepers said, but perhaps they were merely taking advantage of being inviolable, beyond any kings, to jack up prices. Some chiefs, including Loklann, had begun to experiment with hydrogen production for themselves, but it was a slow thing to puzzle out an art that even the Keepers only half understood.)

Here, strong men replaced machinery. The *Buffalo* was soon pegged down in the cathedral plaza, which it almost filled. Loklann inspected each rope himself. His wounded leg ached, but not too badly to walk on. More annoying was his right arm, which hurt worse from stitches than from the original cut. The medic had warned him to go easy with it. That meant fighting left-handed, for the story should never be told that Loklann sunna Holber stayed out of combat. However, he would only be half himself.

He touched the knife which had spiked him. At least he'd gotten a fine steel blade for his pains. And . . . hadn't the owner said they would meet again, to settle who kept it? There were omens in such words. It could be a pleasure to reincarnate that Ruori.

"Skipper. Skipper, sir."

Loklann glanced about. Yuw Red-Ax and Aalan sunna Rickar, men of his lodge, had hailed him. They grasped the arms of a young woman in black velvet and silver. The beweaponed crowd, moiling about, was focusing on her; raw whoops lifted over the babble.

"What is it?" said Loklann brusquely. He had much to do.

"This wench, sir. A looker, isn't she? We found her down near the waterfront."

"Well, shove her into the temple with the rest till —oh." Loklann rocked back on his heels, narrowing his eyes to meet a steady green glare. She was certainly a looker.

"She kept hollering the same words over and over: *'Shef, rey, ombro gran.'* I finally wondered if it didn't mean 'chief,'" said Yuw, "and then when she yelled 'khan' I was pretty sure she wanted to see you. So we didn't use her ourselves," he finished virtuously.

"Aba tu Spañol?" said the girl.

Loklann grinned. "Yes," he replied in the same language, his words heavily accented but sufficient. "Well enough to know you are calling me 'thou.'" Her pleasantly formed mouth drew into a thin line. "Which means you think I am your inferior—or your god, or your beloved.''

She flushed, threw back her head (sunlight ran along crow's-wing hair) and answered: "You might tell these oafs to release me."

Loklann said the order in Angliz. Yuw and Aalan let go. The marks of their fingers were bruised into her arms. Loklann stroked his beard. "Did you want to see me?" he asked.

"If you are the leader, yes," she said. "I am the calde's daughter, Doñita Tresa Carabán." Briefly, her voice wavered. "That is my father's chain of office you are wearing. I came back on behalf of his people, to ask for terms."

"What?" Loklann blinked. Someone in the warrior crowd laughed.

It must not be in her to beg mercy, he thought; her tone remained brittle. "Considering your sure losses if you fight to a finish, and the chance of provoking a counterattack on your homeland, will you not accept a money ransom and a safe-conduct, releasing your captives and ceasing your destruction?"

"By Oktai," murmured Loklann. "Only a woman could imagine we—" He stopped. "Did you say you came back?"

She nodded. "On the people's behalf. I know I have no legal authority to make terms, but in practice—"

"Forget that!" he rapped. "Where did you come back from?"

She faltered. "That has nothing to do with—"

There were too many eyes around. Loklann bawled orders to start systematic plundering. He turned to the girl. "Come aboard the airship," he said. "I want to discuss this further.''

Her eyes closed, for just a moment, and her lips moved. Then she looked at him—he thought of a cougar he had once trapped—and she said in a flat voice: ''Yes. I do have more arguments.''

''Any woman does,'' he laughed, ''but you better than most.''

''Not that!'' she flared. ''I meant—no. Marí, pray for me.'' As he pushed a way through his men, she followed him.

They went past furled sails, to a ladder let down from the gallery. A hatch stood open to the lower hull, showing storage space and leather fetters for slaves. A few guards were posted on the gallery deck. They leaned on their weapons, sweating from beneath helmets, swapping jokes; when Loklann led the girl by, they yelled good-humored envy.

He opened a door. ''Have you ever seen one of our vessels?'' he asked. The upper gondola contained a long room, bare except for bunk frames on which sleeping bags were laid. Beyond, a series of partitions defined cabinets, a sort of galley, and at last, in the very bow, a room for maps, tables, navigation instruments, speaking tubes. Its walls slanted so far outward that the glazed windows would give a spacious view when the ship was aloft. On a shelf, beneath racked weapons, sat a small idol, tusked and four-armed. A pallet was rolled on the floor.

''The bridge,'' said Loklann. ''Also the captain's cabin.'' He gestured at one of four wicker chairs, lashed into place. ''Be seated, Doñita. Would you like something to drink?''

She sat down but did not reply. Her fists were

clenched on her lap. Loklann poured himself a slug of
whiskey and tossed off half at a gulp. "Ahhh! Later
we will get some of your own wine for you. It is a
shame you have no art of distilling here."

Desperate eyes lifted to him, where he stood over
her. "S'ñor," she said, "I beg of you, in Carito's
name—well, in your mother's, then—spare my people."

"My mother would laugh herself ill to hear that,"
he said. Leaning forward: "See here, let us not spill
words. You were escaping, but you came back.
Where were you escaping to?"

"I—does that matter?"

Good, he thought, she was starting to crack. He
hammered: "It does. I know you were at the palace
this dawn. I know you fled with the dark foreigners. I
know their ship departed an hour ago. You must
have been on it, but left again. True?"

"Yes." She began to tremble.

He sipped molten fire and asked reasonably:
"Now, tell me, Doñita, what you have to bargain
with. You cannot have expected we would give up
the best part of our booty and a great many valuable
slaves for a mere safe-conduct. All the Sky kingdoms
would disown us. Come now, you must have more to
offer, if you hope to buy us off."

"No . . . not really—"

His hand exploded against her cheek. Her head
jerked from the blow. She huddled back, touching
the red mark, as he growled: "I have no time for
games. Tell me! Tell me this instant what thought
drove you back here from safety, or down in the hold
you go. You'd fetch a good price when the traders

next visit Canyon. Many homes are waiting for you: a woods runner's cabin in Orgon, a Mong khan's yurt in Tekkas, a brothel as far east as Chai Ka-Go. Tell me now, truly, what you know, and you will be spared that much.''

She looked downward and said raggedly: "The foreign ship is loaded with the calde's gold. My father had long wanted to remove his personal treasure to a safer place than this, but dared not risk a wagon train across country. There are still many outlaws between here and Fortlez d' S' Ernán; that much loot would tempt the military escort itself to turn bandit. Captain Lohannaso agreed to carry the gold by sea to Port Wanawato, which is near Fortlez. He could be trusted because his government is anxious for trade with us; he came here officially. The treasure had already been loaded. Of course, when your raid came, the ship also took those women who had been at the palace. But can you not spare them? You'll find more loot in the foreign ship than your whole fleet can lift.''

"By Oktai!" whispered Loklann.

He turned from her, paced, finally stopped and stared out the window. He could almost hear the gears turn in his head. It made sense. The palace had been disappointing. Oh, yes, a lot of damask and silverware and whatnot, but nothing like the cathedral. Either the calde was less rich than powerful, or he concealed his hoard. Loklann had planned to torture a few servants and find out which. Now he realized there was a third possibility.

Better interrogate some prisoners anyway, to make sure—no, no time. Given a favoring wind, that ship

could outrun any rover without working up a sweat.
It might already be too late to overhaul. But if not—
h'm. Assault would be no cinch. That lean, pitching
hull was a small target for paratroops, and with rigging in the way . . . Wait. Bold men could always
find a road. How about grappling to the upper
works? If the strain tore the rigging loose, so much
the better: a weighted rope would then give a clear
slideway to the deck. If the hooks held, though, a
storming party could nevertheless go along the lines,
into the topmasts. Doubtless the sailors were agile
too, but had they ever reefed a rover sail in a Merikan
thunderstorm, a mile above the earth?

He could improvise as the battle developed. At the
very least, it would be fun to try. And at most, he
might be reborn a world conqueror, for such an exploit in this life.

He laughed aloud, joyously. "We'll do it!"

Tresa rose. "You will spare the city?" she whispered hoarsely.

"I never promised any such thing," said Loklann.
"Of course, the ship's cargo will crowd out most of
the stuff and people we might take otherwise.
Unless, hm, unless we decide to sail the ship to Cal-
forni, loaded, and meet it there with more rovers.
Yes, why not?"

"You oathbreaker," she said, with a hellful of
scorn.

"I only promised not to sell you," said Loklann.
His gaze went up and down her. "And I won't."

He took a stride forward and gathered her to him.
She fought, cursing; once she managed to draw
Ruori's knife from his belt, but his cuirass stopped
the blade.

Finally he rose. She wept at his feet, her breast marked red by her father's chain. He said more quietly, "No, I will not sell you, Tresa. I will keep you."

"Blimp ho-o-o-!"

The lookout's cry hung lonesome for a minute between wind and broad waters. Down under the mainmast, it seethed with crewmen running to their posts.

Ruori squinted eastward. The land was a streak under cumulus clouds, mountainous and blue-shadowed. It took him a while to find the enemy, in all that sky. At last the sun struck them. He lifted his binoculars. Two painted killer whales lazed his way, slanting down from a mile altitude.

He sighed. "Only two," he said.

"That may be more than plenty for us," said Atel Hamid. Sweat studded his forehead.

Ruori gave his mate a sharp look. "You're not afraid of them, are you? I daresay that's been one of their biggest assets, superstition."

"Oh, no, Captain. I know the principle of buoyancy as well as you do. But those people are tough. And they're not trying to storm us from a dock this time; they're in their element."

"So are we." Ruori clapped the other man's back. "Take over. Tanaroa knows what's going to happen, but use your own judgment if I'm spitted."

"I wish you'd let me go," protested Atel. "I don't like being safe here. It's what can happen aloft that worries me."

"You won't be too safe for your liking." Ruori

forced a grin. "And somebody has to steer this tub home to hand in those lovely reports to the Geoethnic Research Endeavor."

He swung down the ladder to the main deck and hurried to the mainmast shrouds. His crew yelled around him, weapons gleamed. The two big box kites quivered taut canvas, lashed to a bollard and waiting. Ruori wished there had been time to make more.

Even as it was, though, he had delayed longer than seemed wise, first heading far out to sea and then tacking slowly back, to make the enemy search for him while he prepared. (Or planned, for that matter. When he dismissed Tresa, his ideas had been little more than a conviction that he could fight.) Assuming they were lured after him at all, he had risked their losing patience and going back to the land. For an hour, now, he had dawdled under mainsail, genoa, and a couple of flying jibs, hoping the Sky People were lubbers enough not to find that suspiciously little canvas for this good weather.

But here they were, and here was an end to worry and remorse on a certain girl's behalf. Such emotions were rare in an Islander; and to find himself focusing them thus on a single person, out of earth's millions, had been horrible. Ruori swarmed up the ratlines, as if he fled something.

The blimps were still high, passing overhead on an upper-level breeze. Down here was almost a straight south wind. The aircraft, unable to steer really close-hauled, would descend when they were sea-level upwind of him. Regardless, estimated a cold part of Ruori, the *Dolphin* could avoid their clumsy rush.

But the *Dolphin* wasn't going to.

The rigging was now knotted with armed sailors.

Ruori pulled himself onto the mainmast crosstrees and sat down, casually swinging his legs. The ship heeled over in a flaw and he hung above greenish-blue, white-streaked immensity. He balanced, scarcely noticing, and asked Hiti: "Are you set?"

"Aye." The big harpooner, his body a writhe of tattoos and muscles, nodded a shaven head. Lashed to the fid where he squatted was the ship's catapult, cocked and loaded with one of the huge irons that could kill a sperm whale at a blow. A couple more lay alongside in their rack. Hiti's two mates and four deckhands poised behind him, holding the smaller harpoons—mere six-foot shafts—that were launched from a boat by hand. The lines of all trailed down the mast to the bows.

"Aye, let 'em come now." Hiti grinned over his whole round face. "Nan eat the world, but this'll be something to make a dance about when we come home!"

"If we do," said Ruori. He touched the boat ax thrust into his loincloth. Like a curtain, the blinding day seemed to veil a picture from home, where combers broke white under the moon, longfires flared on a beach and dancers were merry, and palm trees cast shadows for couples who stole away. He wondered how a Meycan calde's daughter might like it . . . if her throat had not been cut.

"There's a sadness on you, Captain," said Hiti.

"Men are going to die," said Ruori.

"What of it?" Small kindly eyes studied him. "They'll die willing, if they must, for the sake of the song that'll be made. You've another trouble than death."

"Let me be!"

The harpooner looked hurt, but withdrew into silence. Wind streamed and the ocean glittered.

The aircraft steered close. They would approach one on each side. Ruori unslung the megaphone at his shoulder. Atel Hamid held the *Dolphin* steady on a broad reach.

Now Ruori could see a grinning god at the prow of the starboard airship. It would pass just above the topmasts, a little to windward . . . Arrows went impulsively toward it from the yardarms, without effect, but no one was excited enough to waste a rifle cartridge. Hiti swiveled his catapult. "Wait," said Ruori. "We'd better see what they do."

Helmeted heads appeared over the blimp's gallery rail. A man stepped up—another, another, at intervals; they whirled triple-clawed iron grapnels and let go. Ruori saw one strike the foremast, rebound, hit a jib . . . . The line to the blimp tautened and sang but did not break; it was of leather . . . . The jib ripped, canvas thundered, struck a sailor in the belly and knocked him from his yard . . . . The man recovered to straighten out and hit the water in a clean dive. Lesu grant he lived . . . . The grapnel bumped along, caught the gaff of the fore-and-aft mainsail, wood groaned . . . . The ship trembled as line after line snapped tight.

She leaned far over, dragged by leverage. Her sails banged. No danger of capsizing—yet—but a mast could be pulled loose. And now, over the gallery rail and seizing a rope between hands and knees, the pirates came. Whooping like boys, they slid down to the grapnels and clutched after any rigging that came to hand.

One of them sprang monkeylike onto the main-mast gaff, below the crosstrees. A harpooner's mate cursed, hurled his weapon, and skewered the invader. "Belay that!" roared Hiti. "We need those irons!"

Ruori scanned the situation. The leeward blimp was still maneuvering in around its mate, which was being blown to port. He put the megaphone to his mouth and a solar-battery amplifier cried for him. "Hear this! Hear this! Burn that second enemy now, before he grapples! Cut the lines to the first one and repel all boarders!"

"Shall I fire?" called Hiti. "I'll never have a better target."

"Aye."

The harpooner triggered his catapult. It unwound with a thunder noise. Barbed steel smote the engaged gondola low in a side, tore through, and ended on the far side of interior planking.

"Wind 'er up!" bawled Hiti. His own gorilla hands were already on a crank lever. Somehow two men found space to help him.

Ruori slipped down the futtock shrouds and jumped to the gaff. Another pirate had landed there and a third was just arriving, two more aslide behind him. The man on the spar balanced barefooted, as good as any sailor, and drew a sword. Ruori dropped as the blade whistled, caught a mainsail grommet one-handed, and hung there, striking with his boat ax at the grapnel line. The pirate crouched and stabbed at him. Ruori thought of Tresa, smashed his hatchet into the man's face, and flipped him off, down to the deck. He cut again. The leather was tough, but his blade was keen. The line parted and whipped away. The gaff swung free, almost yanking Ruori's fingers loose. The second Sky Man toppled, hit a cabin below and spattered. The men on the line slid to its end. One of them could not stop; the sea took him. The other was smashed against the masthead as he pendulumed.

Ruori pulled himself back astride the gaff and sat there awhile, heaving air into lungs that burned. The fight ramped around him, on shrouds and spars and down on the decks. The second blimp edged closer.

Astern, raised by the speed of a ship moving into the wind, a box kite lifted. Atel sang a command and the helmsman put the rudder over. Even with the drag on her, the *Dolphin* responded well; a profound science of fluid mechanics had gone into her design. Being soaked in whale oil, the kite clung to the gas bag for a time—long enough for "messengers" of burning paper to whirl up its string. It burst into flame.

The blimp sheered off, the kite fell away, its small gunpowder load exploded harmlessly. Atel swore and gave further orders. The *Dolphin* tacked. The second kite, already aloft and afire, hit target. It detonated.

Hydrogen gushed out. Sudden flames wreathed the blimp. They seemed pale in the sun-dazzle. Smoke began to rise, as the plastic between gas cells disintegrated. The aircraft descended like a slow meteorite to the water.

Its companion vessel had no reasonable choice but to cast loose unsevered grapnels, abandoning the still outnumbered boarding party. The captain could not know that the *Dolphin* had only possessed two kites. A few vengeful catapult bolts spat from it. Then it was free, rapidly falling astern. The Maurai ship rocked toward an even keel.

The enemy might retreat or he might plan some fresh attack. Ruori did not intend that it should be either. He megaphoned: "Put about! Face that scum-gut!" and led a rush down the shrouds to a deck where combat still went on.

For Hiti's gang had put three primary harpoons and half a dozen lesser ones into the gondola.

Their lines trailed in tightening catenaries from the blimp to the capstan in the bows. No fear now of undue strain. The *Dolphin*, like any Maurai craft, was meant to live off the sea as she traveled. She had dragged right whales alongside; a blimp was nothing in comparison. What counted was speed, before the pirates realized what was happening and found ways to cut loose.

"Tohiha, hioha, itoki, itoki!" The old canoe chant rang forth as men tramped about the capstan. Ruori hit the deck, saw a Canyon man fighting a sailor, sword against club, and brained the fellow from behind as he would any other vermin. (Then he wondered, dimly shocked, what made him think thus about a human being.) The battle was rapidly concluded; the Sky Men faced hopeless odds. But half a dozen Federation people were badly hurt. Ruori had the few surviving pirates tossed into a lazaret, his own casualties taken below to anesthetics and antibiotics and cooing Doñitas. Then, quickly, he prepared his crew for the next phase.

The blimp had been drawn almost to the bowsprit. It was canted over so far that its catapults were useless. Pirates lined the gallery deck, howled and shook

their weapons. They outnumbered the *Dolphin* crew
by a factor of three or four. Ruori recognized one
among them—the tall yellow-haired man who had
fought him outside the palace; it was a somehow
eerie feeling.

"Shall we burn them?" asked Atel.

Ruori grimaced. "I suppose we have to," he said.
"Try not to ignite the vessel itself. You know we
want it."

A walking beam moved up and down, driven by
husky Islanders. Flame spurted from a ceramic
nozzle. The smoke and stench and screams that
followed, and the things to be seen when Ruori
ordered cease fire, made the hardest veteran of corsair
patrol look a bit ill. The Maurai were an unsenti-
mental folk, but they did not like to inflict pain.

"Hose," rasped Ruori. The streams of water that
followed were like some kind of blessing. Wicker that
had begun to burn hissed into charred quiescence.

The ship's grapnels were flung. A couple of cabin
boys darted past grown men to be first along the
lines. They met no resistance on the gallery. The un-
injured majority of pirates stood in a numb fashion,
their armament at their feet, the fight kicked out of
them. Jacob's ladders followed the boys; the *Dolphin*
crew swarmed aboard the blimp and started collect-
ing prisoners.

A few Sky Men lurched from behind a door, weapons aloft. Ruori saw the tall fair man among them.
The man drew Ruori's dagger, left-handed, and ran
toward him. His right arm seemed nearly useless. "A
Canyon, a Canyon!" he called, the ghost of a war cry.

Ruori sidestepped the charge and put out a foot.
The blond man tripped. As he fell, the hammer of

Ruori's ax clopped down, catching him on the neck. He crashed, tried to rise, shuddered, and lay twitching.

"I want my knife back." Ruori squatted, undid the robber's tooled leather belt, and began to hogtie him.

Dazed blue eyes looked up with a sort of pleading. "Are you not going to kill me?" mumbled the other in Spañol.

"Haristi, no," said Ruori, surprised. "Why should I?"

He sprang erect. The last resistance had ended; the blimp was his. He opened the forward door, thinking the equivalent of a ship's bridge must lie beyond it.

Then for a while he did not move at all, nor did he hear anything but the wind and his own blood.

It was Tresa who finally came to him. Her hands were held out before her, like a blind person's, and her eyes looked through him. "You are here," she said, flat and empty voiced.

"Doñita," stammered Ruori. He caught her hands. "Doñita, had I known you were aboard, I would never have . . . have risked—"

"Why did you not burn and sink us, like that other vessel?" she asked. "Why must this return to the city?"

She wrenched free of him and stumbled out onto the deck. It was steeply tilted, and bucked beneath her. She fell, picked herself up, walked with barefoot care to the rail and stared out across the ocean. Her hair and torn dress fluttered in the wind.

There was a great deal of technique to handling an airship. Ruori could feel that the thirty men he had put aboard this craft were sailing it as awkwardly as possible. An experienced Sky Man would know what sort of thermals and downdrafts to expect, just from a glance at land or water below; he could estimate the level at which a desired breeze was blowing, and rise or fall smoothly; he could even beat to windward, though that would be a slow process much plagued by drift.

Nevertheless, an hour's study showed the basic principles. Ruori went back to the bridge and gave orders in the speaking tube. Presently the land came nearer. A glance below showed the *Dolphin*, with a cargo of war captives, following on shortened sail. He and his fellow aeronauts would have to take a lot of banter about their celestial snail's pace. Ruori did not smile at the thought or plan his replies, as he would have done yesterday. Tresa sat so still behind him.

"Do you know the name of this craft, Doñita?" he asked, to break the silence.

"He called it *Buffalo*," she said, remote and un-interested.

"What's that?"

"A sort of wild cattle."

"I gather, then, he talked to you while cruising in search of me. Did he say anything else of interest?"

"He spoke of his people. He boasted of the things they have which we don't . . . engines, powers, alloys . . . as if that made them any less a pack of filthy savages."

At least she was showing some spirit. He had been afraid she had started willing her heart to stop; but he remembered he had seen no evidence of that common Maurai practice here in Meyco.

"Did he abuse you badly?" he asked, not looking at her.

"You would not consider it abuse," she said violently. "Now leave me alone, for mercy's sake!" He heard her go from him, through the door to the after sections.

Well, he thought, after all, her father was killed. That would grieve anyone, anywhere in the world, but her perhaps more than him. For a Meycan child was raised solely by its parents; it did not spend half its time eating or sleeping or playing with any casual relative, like most Island young. So the immediate kin would have more psychological significance here. At least, this was the only explanation Ruori could think of for the sudden darkness within Tresa.

The city hove into view. He saw the remaining enemy vessels gleam above. Three against one . . . yes, today would become a legend among the Sea People, if he succeeded. Ruori knew he should have felt the same reckless pleasure as a man did surf-bathing, or shark fighting, or sailing in a typhoon, any breakneck sport where success meant glory and girls. He could hear his men chant, beat war-drum rhythms out with hands and stamping feet. But his own heart was Antarctic.

The nearest hostile craft approached. Ruori tried to meet it in a professional way. He had attired his prize crew in captured Sky outfits. A superficial glance would take them for legitimate Canyonites, depleted after a hard fight but the captured Maurai ship at their heels.

As the northerners steered close in the leisurely airship fashion, Ruori picked up his speaking tube. "Steady as she goes. Fire when we pass abeam."

"Aye, aye," said Hiti.

A minute later the captain heard the harpoon catapult rumble. Through a port he saw the missile strike the enemy gondola amidships. "Pay out line," he said. "We want to hold her for the kite, but not get burned ourselves."

"Aye, I've played swordfish before now." Laughter bubbled in Hiti's tones.

The foe sheered, frantic. A few bolts leaped from its catapults; one struck home, but a single punctured gas cell made slight difference. "Put about!" cried Ruori. No sense in presenting his beam to a broadside. Both craft began to drift downwind, sails flapping. "Hard alee!" The *Buffalo* became a drogue, holding its victim to a crawl. And here came the kite prepared on the way back. This time it included fish hooks. It caught and held fairly on the Canyonite bag. "Cast off!" yelled Ruori. Fire whirled along the kite string. In minutes it had enveloped the enemy. A few parachutes were blown out to sea.

"Two to go," said Ruori, without any of his men's shouted triumph.

The invaders were no fools. Their remaining blimps turned back over the city, not wishing to expose themselves to more flame from the water. One descended, dropped hawsers, and was rapidly hauled to the plaza. Through his binoculars, Ruori saw armed men swarm aboard it. The other, doubtless with a mere patrol crew, maneuvered toward the approaching *Buffalo*.

"I think that fellow wants to engage us," warned Hiti. "Meanwhile number two down yonder will take on a couple of hundred soldiers, then lay alongside us and board."

"I know," said Ruori. "Let's oblige them."

He steered as if to close with the sparsely manned patroller. It did not avoid him, as he had feared it might; but then, there was a compulsive bravery in the Sky culture. Instead, it maneuvered to grapple as quickly as possible. That would give its companion a chance to load warriors and rise. It came very near.

Now to throw a scare in them, Ruori decided. "Fire arrows," he said. Out on deck, hardwood pistons were shoved into little cylinders, igniting tinder at the bottom; thus oil-soaked shafts were kindled. As the enemy came in range, red comets began to streak from the *Buffalo* archers.

Had his scheme not worked, Ruori would have turned off. He didn't want to sacrifice more men in hand-to-hand fighting; instead, he would have tried seriously to burn the hostile airship from afar, though his strategy needed it. But the morale effect of the previous disaster was very much present. As blazing arrows thunked into their gondola, a battle tactic so two-edged that no northern crew was even equipped for it, the Canyonites panicked and went over the side. Perhaps, as they parachuted down, a few noticed that no shafts had been aimed at their gas bag.

"Grab fast!" sang Ruori. "Douse any fires!"

Grapnels thumbed home. The blimps rocked to a relative halt. Men leaped to the adjacent gallery; bucketsful of water splashed.

"Stand by," said Ruori. "Half our boys on the

prize. Break out the lifelines and make them fast.''

He put down the tube. A door squeaked behind him. He turned, as Tresa reentered the bridge. She was still pale, but she had combed her hair, and her head was high.

''Another!'' she said with a note near joy. ''Only one of them left!''

''But it will be full of their men.'' Ruori scowled. ''I wish now I had not accepted your refusal to go aboard the *Dolphin*. I wasn't thinking clearly. This is too hazardous.''

''Do you think I care for that?'' she said. ''I am a Carabán.''

''But I care,'' he said.

The haughtiness dropped from her; she touched his hand, fleetingly, and color rose in her cheeks. ''Forgive me. You have done so much for us. There is no way we can ever thank you.''

''Yes, there is,'' said Ruori.

''Name it.''

''Do not stop your heart just because it has been wounded.''

She looked at him with a kind of sunrise in her eyes.

His boatswain appeared at the outer door. ''All set, Captain. We're holding steady at a thousand feet, a man standing by every valve these two crates have got.''

''Each has been assigned a particular escape line?''

''Aye.'' The boatswain departed.

''You'll need one too. Come.'' Ruori took Tresa by the hand and led her onto the gallery. They saw sky around them, a breeze touched their faces and the deck underfoot moved like a live thing. He indicated many light cords from the *Dolphin*'s store, bowlined to the rail. "We aren't going to risk parachuting with untrained men," he said. "But you've no experience in skinning down one of these. I'll make you a harness which will hold you safely. Ease yourself down hand over hand. When you reach the ground, cut loose." His knife slashed some pieces of rope and he knotted them together with a seaman's skill. When he fitted the harness on her, she grew tense under his fingers.

"But I am your friend," he murmured.

She eased. She even smiled, shakenly. He gave her his knife and went back inboard.

And now the last pirate vessel stood up from the earth. It moved near; Ruori's two craft made no attempt to flee. He saw sunlight flash on edged metal. He knew they had witnessed the end of their companion craft and would not be daunted by the same technique. Rather, they would close in, even while their ship burned about them. If nothing else, they could kindle him in turn and then parachute to safety. He did not send arrows.

When only a few fathoms separated him from the enemy, he cried: "Let go the valves!"

Gas whoofed from both bags. The linked blimps dropped.

"Fire!" shouted Ruori. Hiti aimed his catapult and sent a harpoon with anchor cable through the bottom of the attacker. "Burn and abandon!"

Men on deck touched off oil which other men splashed from jars. Flames sprang high.

With the weight of two nearly deflated vessels

dragging it from below, the Canyon ship began to fall. At five hundred feet the tossed lifelines draped across flat rooftops and trailed in the streets. Ruori went over the side. He scorched his palms going down.

He was not much too quick. The harpooned blimp released compressed hydrogen and rose to a thousand feet with its burden, seeking sky room. Presumably no one had yet seen that the burden was on fire. In no case would they find it easy to shake or cut loose from one of Hiti's irons.

Ruori stared upward. Fanned by the wind, the blaze was smokeless, a small fierce sun. He had not counted on his fire taking the enemy by total surprise. He had assumed they would parachute to earth, where the Meycans could attack. Almost, he wanted to warn them.

Then flame reached the remaining hydrogen in the collapsed gas bags. He heard a sort of giant gasp. The topmost vessel became a flying pyre. The wind bore it out over the city walls. A few antlike figures managed to spring free. The parachute of one was burning.

"Sant'sima Marí," whispered a voice, and Tresa crept into Ruori's arms and hid her face.

After dark, candles were lit throughout the palace. They could not blank the ugliness of stripped walls and smoke-blackened ceilings. The guardsmen who lined the throne room were tattered and weary. Nor did S' Antón itself rejoice, yet. There were too many dead.

Ruori sat throned on the calde's dais, Tresa at his right and Páwolo Dónoju on his left. Until a new set of officials could be chosen, these must take authority. The Don sat rigid, not allowing his bandaged head to droop; but now and then his lids grew too heavy to hold up. Tresa watched enormous-eyed from beneath the hood of a cloak wrapping her. Ruori sprawled at ease, a little more happy now that the fighting was over.

It had been a grim business, even after the heart-ened city troops had sallied and driven the surviving enemy before them. Too many Sky Men fought till they were killed. The hundreds of prisoners, mostly from the first Maurai success, would prove a dangerous booty; no one was sure what to do with them.

"But at least their host is done for," said Dónoju.

Ruori shook his head. "No, S'ñor. I am sorry, but you have no end in sight. Up north are thousands of such aircraft, and a strong hungry people. They will come again."

"We will meet them, Captain. The next time we shall be prepared. A larger garrison, barrage balloons, fire kites, cannons that shoot upward, perhaps a flying navy of our own . . . we can learn what to do."

Tresa stirred. Her tone bore life again, though a life which hated. "In the end, we will carry the war to them. Not one will remain in all the Corado high-lands."

"No," said Ruori. "That must not be."

Her head jerked about; she stared at him from the shadow of her hood. Finally she said, "True, we are bidden to love our enemies, but you cannot mean the

Sky People. They are not human!"

Ruori spoke to a page. "Send for the chief prisoner."

"To hear our judgment on him?" asked Dónoju. "That should be done formally, in public."

"Only to talk with us," said Ruori.

"I do not understand you," said Tresa. Her words faltered, unable to carry the intended scorn. "After everything you have done, suddenly there is no manhood in you."

He wondered why it should hurt for her to say that. He would not have cared if she had been anyone else.

Loklann entered between two guards. His hands were tied behind him and dried blood was on his face, but he walked like a conqueror under the pikes. When he reached the dais, he stood, legs braced apart, and grinned at Tresa.

"Well," he said, "so you find these others less satisfactory and want me back."

She jumped to her feet and screamed: "Kill him!"

"No!" cried Ruori.

The guardsmen hesitated, machetes half drawn. Ruori stood up and caught the girl's wrists. She struggled, spitting like a cat. "Don't kill him, then," she agreed at last, so thickly it was hard to understand. "Not now. Make it slow. Strangle him, burn him alive, toss him on your spears—"

Ruori held fast till she stood quietly.

When he let go, she sat down and wept.

Páwolo Dónoju said in a voice like steel: "I believe I understand. A fit punishment must certainly be devised."

Loklann spat on the floor. "Of course," he said. "When you have a man bound, you can play any number of dirty little games with him."

"Be still," said Ruori. "You are not helping your own cause. Or mine."

He sat down, crossed his legs, laced fingers around a knee, and gazed before him, into the darkness at the hall's end. "I know you have suffered from this man's work," he said carefully. "You can expect to suffer more from his kinfolk in the future. They are a young race, heedless as children, even as your ancestors and mine were once young. Do you think the Perio was established without hurt and harm? Or, if I remember your history rightly, that the Spañol people were welcomed here by the Inios? That the Ingliss did not come to N'Zealann with slaughter, and that the Maurai were not formerly cannibals? In an age of heroes, the hero must have an opponent.

"Your real weapon against the Sky People is not an army, sent to lose itself in unmapped mountains . . . . Your priests, merchants, artists, craftsmen, manners, fashions, learning—there is the means to bring them to you on their knees, if you will use it."

Loklann started. "You devil," he whispered. "Do you actually think to convert us to . . . a woman's faith and a city's cage?" He shook back his tawny mane and roared till the walls rung. "No!"

"It will take a century or two," said Ruori.

Don Páwolo smiled in his young scanty beard. "A refined revenge, S'ñor Captain," he admitted.

"Too refined!" Tresa lifted her face from her hands, gulped after air, held up claw-crooked fingers and brought them down as if into Loklann's eyes. "Even if it could be done," she snarled, "even if they did have souls, what do we want with them, or their children or grandchildren . . . they who murdered our babies today? Before almighty Dío—I am the last Carabán and I will have my following to speak for me in Meyco—there will never be anything for them but extermination. We can do it, I swear. Many Tekkans would help, for plunder. I shall yet live to see your home burning, you swine, and your sons hunted with dogs."

She turned frantically toward Ruori. "How else can our land be safe? We are ringed in by enemies. We have no choice but to destroy them, or they will destroy us. And we are the last Merikan civilization."

She sat back and shuddered. Ruori reached over to take her hand. It felt cold. For an instant, unconsciously, she returned the pressure, then jerked away.

He sighed in his weariness.

"I must disagree," he said. "I am sorry. I realize how you feel."

"You do not," she said through clamped jaws. "You cannot."

"But after all," he said, forcing dryness, "I am not just a man with human desires. I represent my government. I must return to tell them what is here, and I can predict their response.

"They will help you stand off attack. That is not an aid you can refuse, is it? The men who will be responsible for Meyco are not going to decline our offer of alliance merely to preserve a precarious independence of action, whatever a few extremists may argue for. And our terms will be most reasonable. We will want little more from you than a policy working toward conciliation and close relations with the Sky People, as soon as they have tired of battering themselves against our united defense."

"What?" said Loklann. Otherwise the chamber was very still. Eyes gleamed white from the shadows of helmets, toward Ruori.

"We will begin with you," said the Maurai. "At the proper time, you and your fellows will be escorted home. Your ransom will be that your nation allow a diplomatic and trade mission to enter."

"No," said Tresa, as if speech hurt her throat. "Not him. Send back the others if you must, but not him—to boast of what he did today."

Loklann grinned again, looking straight at her. "I will," he said.

Anger flicked in Ruori, but he held his mouth shut.

"I do not understand," hesitated Don Páwolo. "Why do you favor these animals?"

"Because they are more civilized than you," said Ruori.

"What?" The noble sprang to his feet, snatching for his sword. Stiffly, he sat down again. His tone froze over. "Explain yourself, S'ñor."

Ruori could not see Tresa's face, in the private night of her hood, but he felt her drawing farther from him than a star. "They have developed aircraft," he said, slumping back in his chair, worn out and with no sense of victory; *O great creating Tanaroa, grant me sleep this night!*

"But—"

"That was done from the ground up," explained

Ruori, "not as a mere copy of ancient techniques. Beginning as refugees, the Sky People created an agriculture which can send warriors by the thousands from what was desert, yet plainly does not require peon hordes. On interrogation I have learned that they have sunpower and hydroelectric power, a synthetic chemistry of sorts, a well-developed navigation with the mathematics which that implies, gunpowder, metallurgics, aerodynamics. . . . Yes, I daresay it's a lopsided culture, a thin layer of learning above a largely illiterate mass. But even the mass must respect technology, or it would never have been supported to get as far as it has.

"In short," he sighed, wondering if he could make her comprehend, "the Sky People are a scientific race—the only one besides ourselves which we Maurai have yet discovered. And that makes them too precious to lose.

"You have better manners here, more humane laws, higher art, broader vision, every traditional virtue. But you are not scientific. You use rote knowledge handed down from the ancients. Because there is no more fossil fuel, you depend on muscle power; inevitably, then, you have a peon class, and always will. Because the iron and copper mines are exhausted, you tear down old ruins. In your land I have seen no research on wind power, sun power, the energy reserves of the living cell—not to mention the theoretical possibility of hydrogen fusion without a uranium primer. You irrigate the desert at a thousand times the effort it would take to farm the sea, yet have never even tried to improve your fishing techniques. You have not exploited the aluminum which is still abundant in ordinary clays, not sought to make it into strong alloys; no, your farmers use tools of wood and volcanic glass.

"Oh, you are neither ignorant nor superstitious. What you lack is merely the means of gaining new knowledge. You are a fine people; the world is the sweeter for you; I love you as much as I loathe this devil before us. But ultimately, my friends, if left to yourselves, you will slide gracefully back to the Stone Age."

A measure of strength returned. He raised his voice till it filled the hall. "The way of the Sky People is the rough way outward, to the stars. In that respect —and it overrides all others—they are more akin to us Maurai than you are. We cannot let our kin die."

He sat then, in silence, under Loklann's smirk and Dónoju's stare. A guardsman shifted on his feet, with a faint squeak of leather harness.

Tresa said at last, very low in the shadows: "That is your final word, S'ñor?"

"Yes," said Ruori. He turned to her. As she leaned forward, the hood fell back a little, so that candlelight touched her. And the sight of green eyes and parted lips gave him back his victory.

He smiled. "I do not expect you will understand at once. May I discuss it with you again, often? When you have seen the Islands, as I hope you will—"

"You *foreigner!*" she screamed.

Her hand cracked on his cheek. She rose and ran down the dais steps and out of the hall.

PROGRESS

"There they are! Aircraft ho-o-o!"

Keanua's bull bellow came faintly down to Ranu from the crow's nest, almost drowned in the slatting and cracking of sails. He could have spoken clearly head-to-head, but best save that for real emergencies. Otherwise, by some accident, the Brahmards might learn about it.

If they don't already know, Ranu thought.

The day was too bright for what was going to happen. Big, wrinkled waves marched past. Their backs were a hundred different blues, from the color of the sky overhead to a royal midnight; their troughs shaded through gray-amber to a clear green. Foam swirled intricately upon them. Further off they became a single restlessness that glittered with sunlight, on out to the horizon. They rushed and rumbled,

they smacked against the hulls, which rolled somewhat beneath Ranu's feet, making him aware of the
interplay in his leg muscles. The air was mild, but
had a strong thrust and saltiness to it.

Ranu wished he could sink into the day. Nothing
would happen for minutes yet. He should think only
about sunlight warming his skin, wind ruffling his
hair, blue shadows upon an amazingly white cloud
high up where the air was not so swift. Once the
Beneghalis arrived, he might be dead. Keanua, he
felt sure, wasn't worrying about that until the time
came. But then, Keanua was from Taiiti. Ranu had
been born and bred in N'Zealann; his Maurai genes
were too mixed with the old fretful Ingliss. It showed
on his body also, tall and lean, with narrow face and
beaky nose, brown hair and the rarity of blue eyes.

He unslung his binoculars and peered after the
airship. A light touch on his arm recalled him. He
lowered the glasses and smiled lopsidedly at Alisabeta
Kanukauai.

"Still too far to see from here," he told her. "The
topmasts get in the way. But don't bother going
aloft. She'll be overhead before you could swarm
halfway up the shrouds."

The wahine nodded. She was rather short, a trifle
on the stocky side, but because she was young her
figure looked good in the brief lap-lap. A hibiscus
flower from the deck garden adorned her blue-black
locks, which were cut off just below the ears like the
men's. Sailors couldn't be bothered with glamorous
tresses, even on a trimaran as broad and stable as this.
On some ships, of course, a woman had no duties
beyond housekeeping. But Alisabeta was a cyber-

neticist. The Lohannaso Shippers' Association, to which she and Ranu were both related by blood, preferred to minimize crews; so everybody doubled as something else.

That was one reason the *Aorangi* had been picked for this task. The fact of Alisabeta's technical training could not be hidden from the Brahmards. Eyes sharpened by suspicion would see a thousand subtle traces in her manner, left by years of mathematical logic, physics, engineering. But such would be quite natural in a Lohannaso girl.

Moreover, if this job went sour, only three lives would have been sacrificed. Some merchant craft had as many as ten kanakas and three wahines aboard.

"I suppose I'd better get back to the radio," said Alisabeta. "They may want to call."

"I doubt that," said Ranu. "If they aren't simply going to attack us from above, they'll board. They told us they would, when we talked before. But yes, I suppose you had better stand by."

His gaze followed her with considerable pleasure. Usually, in the culture of the Sea People, there was something a little unnatural about a career woman, a female to whom her own home and children were merely incidental if she elected to have them at all. But Alisabeta had been as good a cook, as merry a companion, as much alive in a man's arms on moonlit nights, as any seventeen-year-old signed on to see the world before she settled down. And she was a damned interesting talk-friend, too. Her interpretations of the shaky ethnopolitical situation were so shrewd you might have thought her formally educated in psychodynamics.

I wonder, Ranu said to himself slowly, not for the first time. *Marriage* could *perhaps work out. It's almost unheard of for a sailor, even a skipper, to have a private woman along. And children . . . . But it has been done, once in a while.*

She vanished behind the carved porch screen of the radio shack, on whose vermin-proofed thatch a bougainvillea twined and flared with color. Ranu jerked his mind back to the present. *Time enough to make personal plans if we get out of this alive.*

The airship hove into view. The shark-shaped gasbag was easily a hundred meters long, the control fins spread out like roc's wings. Propeller noise came softly down through the wind. On the flanks was painted the golden Siva symbol of the Brahmard scientocracy: destruction and rebirth.

Rebirth of what? Well, that's what we're here to learn.

The *Aorangi* was drifting before the wind, but not very fast, with her sails and vanes skewed at such lunatic angles. The aircraft paced her easily, losing altitude until it was hardly above deck level, twenty meters away. Ranu saw turbaned heads and high-collared tunics lining the starboard observation verandah. Keanua, who had scrambled down from the crow's nest, hurried to the port rail and placed himself by one of the cargo-loading king posts. He pulled off his shirt—even a Taiitian needed protection against this tropical sea glare, above the shade of the sails—and waved it to attract attention. Ranu saw a man on the flyer nod and issue instructions.

Keanua worked the emergency handwheels. A boom swung out. A catapult in the bow of the airship fired a grapnel. That gunner was good; the hook engaged the cargo sling on the first try. It had two lines attached. Keanua—a thick man with elaborate tattoos on his flat cheerful face—brought the grapnel inboard and made one cable fast. He carried the other one aft and secured it to a bollard at the next king post. With the help of the airship's stern catapult he repeated this process in reverse. The two craft were linked.

For a minute the Beneghali pilot got careless and let the cables draw taut. The *Aorangi* heeled with the drag on her. Sails thundered overhead. Ranu winced at the thought of the stresses imposed on his masts and yards. Ship timber wasn't exactly cheap, even after centuries of good forest management. (Briefly and stingingly he recalled those forests, rustling leaves, sunflecked shadows, a glade that suddenly opened on an enormous vista of downs and grazing sheep and one white waterfall: his father's home.) The aircraft was far less able to take such treatment, and the pilot made haste to adjust its position.

When the configuration was balanced, with the Beneghali vessel several meters aloft, a dozen men slid down a cable. The first came in a bosun's chair arrangement, but the others just wrapped an arm and a leg around the line. Each free hand carried a weapon.

Ranu crossed the deck to meet them. The leader got out of the chair with dignity. He was not tall, but he held himself straight as a rifle barrel. Trousers, tunic, turban were like snow under the sun. His face was sharp, with tight lips in a grizzled beard. He bowed stiffly. "At your service, Captain," he said in

the Beneghali version of Hinji. "Scientist-adminis-
trator Indravarman Dhananda makes you welcome to
these waters." The tone was flat.

Ranu refrained from offering a handshake in the
manner of the Maurai Federation. "Captain Ranu
Karelo Makintairu," he said. Like many sailors, he
spoke fluent Hinji. His companions had acquired the
language in a few weeks' intensive training. They approached, and Ranu introduced them. "Aeromotive
engineer Keanua Filipoa Jouberti; cyberneticist
Alisabeta Kanukauai."

Dhananda's black eyes darted about. "Are there
others?" he asked.

"No," grunted Keanua. "We wouldn't be in this
pickle if we had some extra hands."

The bearded, green-uniformed soldiers had
quietly moved to command the whole deck. Some
stood where they could see no one lurked behind the
cabins. They wasted no admiration on grain of wood,
screens of Okkaidan shoji, or the strong curve of the
roofs. This was an inhumanly businesslike civilization. Ranu noted that besides swords and tele-
scoping pikes, they had two submachine guns.

Yes, he thought with a little chill under his scalp,
*Federation Intelligence made no mistake. Something
very big indeed is hidden on that island.*

Dhananda ceased studying him. It was obvious
that the scantily clad Maurai bore no weapons other
than their knives. "You will forgive our seeming dis-
trustfulness, Captain," the Brahmard said. "But the
Buruma coast is still infested with pirates."

"I know." Ranu made his features smile. "You
see the customary armament emplacements on our
deck."

"Er . . . I understand from your radio call that you are in distress."

"Considerable," said Alisabeta. "Our engine is disabled. Three people cannot possibly trim those sails, and resetting the vanes won't help much."

"What about dropping the sails and going on propellers?" asked Dhananda. His coldness returned. In Beneghal, only women for hire—a curious institution the Maurai knew almost nothing about—traveled freely with men.

"The screws run off the same engine, sir," Alisabeta answered, more demurely than before.

"Well, you can let most of the sails fall, can't you, and stop this drift toward the reefs?"

"Not without smashing our superstructure," Ranu told him. "Synthetic or not, that fabric has a lot of total area. It's *heavy*. Worse, it'd be blown around the decks, fouling gear and breaking cabins. Also, we'd still have extremely poor control." He pointed at the steering wheel aft in the pilothouse, now lashed in place. "The whole rudder system on craft of this type is based on sail and vane adjustment. For instance, with the wind abeam like this, we ought to strip the mainmast and raise the *wanaroa*—oh, never mind. It's a specially curve-battened, semitubular sail with vanes on its yard to redirect airflow aloft. These trimarans have shallow draft and skimpy keel. It makes them fast, but requires exact rigging."

"Mmmmm . . . yes, I think I understand." Dhananda tugged his beard and brooded. "What do you need to make you seaworthy again?"

"A dook and a few days to work," said Alisabeta promptly. "With your help, we should be able to make Port Arberta."

"Um-m-m. There are certain difficulties about that. Could you not get a tow on to the mainland from some other vessel?"

"Not in time," said Ranu. He pointed east, where a shadow lay on the horizon. "We'll be aground in a few more hours if something isn't done."

"You know how little trade comes on this route at this season," Alisabeta added. "Yours was the only response to our SOS, except for a ship near the Nicbars." She paused before continuing with what Ranu hoped was not overdone casualness: "That ship promised to inform our Association of our whereabouts. Her captain assumed a Beneghali patrol would help us put into Arberta for repairs."

She was not being altogether untruthful. Ships did lie at Car Nicbar—camouflaged sea and aircraft, waiting. But they were hours distant.

Dhananda was not silent long. Whatever decision the Brahmard had made, it came with a swiftness and firmness that Ranu admired. (Though such qualities were not to be wished for in an enemy, were they?) "Very well," he yielded, rather sourly. "We shall assist you into harbor and see that the necessary work is completed. You can also radio the mainland that you will be late. Where are you bound?"

"Calcut," said Ranu. "Wool, hides, preserved fish, timber, and algal oils."

"You are from N'Zealann, then," Dhananda concluded.

"Yes. Wellantoa registry. Uh, I'm being inhospitable. Can we not offer the honorable scientist refreshment?"

"Later. Let us get started first."

That took an hour or so. The Beneghalis were land-lubbers. But they could pull strongly on a line at Keanua's direction. So the plasticloth was lowered, slowly and awkwardly, folded and stowed. A couple of studding sails and jibs were left up, a spanker and flowsail were raised, the vanes were adjusted, and the ship began responding somewhat to her rudder. The aircraft paced alongside, still attached. It was far too lightly built, of wicker and fabric, to serve as a drogue; but it helped modify the wind pattern. With her crabwise motion toward the reefs halted, the *Aorangi* limped landward.

Ranu took Dhananda on a guided tour. Few Hinjan countries carried an ocean-borne trade. Their merchants went overland by camel caravan or sent high-priced perishables by air. The Brahmard had never been aboard one of the great vessels that bound together the Maurai Federation, from Awaii in the west to N'Zealann in the south, and carried the Cross and Stars flag around the planet. He was clearly looking for concealed weapons and spies in the woodwork. But he was also interested in the ship for her own sake.

"I am used to schooners and junks and the like," he said. "This looks radical."

"It's a rather new design," Ranu agreed. "But more are being built. You'll see many in the future."

With most sails down, the deck had taken on an austere appearance. Only the cabins, the hatches and king posts, cleats and bollards and defense installations, the sunpower collectors forward, and Keanua's flower garden broke that wide sweep. The three hulls were hidden beneath it, except where the prows jutted forth, bearing extravagantly carved tiki figureheads. There were three masts. Those fore and aft were more or less conventional; the mainmast was a tripod, wrought to withstand tremendous forces. Dhananda admitted he was bewildered by the variety of yards and lines hanging against the sky.

"We trim exactly, according to wind and current," Ranu explained. "Continuous measurements are taken by automatic instruments. A computer below decks calculates what's necessary, and directs the engine in the work."

"I know aerodynamics and hydrodynamics are thoroughly developed disciplines," the Beneghali said, impressed. "Large modern aircraft couldn't move about on such relatively feeble motors as they have unless they were designed with great care. But I had not appreciated the extent to which the same principles are being applied to marine architecture." He sighed. "That is one basic trouble with the world today, Captain. Miserably slow communications. Yes, one can send a radio signal, or cross the ocean in days if the weather is favorable. But so few people do it. The volume of talk and traffic is so small. An invention like this ship can exist for decades before anyone outside its own country is really aware of it. The benefits are denied to more remote people for . . . generations, sometimes."

He seemed to recognize the intensity that had crept into his voice, and broke off.

"Oh, I don't know," said Ranu. "International improvement does go on. Two hundred years ago, say, my ancestors were fooling around with multimasted hermaphrodite craft, and the Mericans used sails and fan keels on their blimps—with no anti-catalyst for the hydrogen! Can you imagine such a firetrap? At the same time, if you'll pardon my saying so, the Hinjan subcontinent was a howling chaos of folk migrations. You couldn't have used even those square-rigger blimps, if someone had offered them to you."

"What has that to do with my remarks?" Dhananda asked, bridling.

"Just that I believe the Maurai government is right in advocating that the world go slow in making changes," said Ranu. He was being deliberately provocative, hoping to get a hint of how far things had gone on South Annaman. But Dhananda only shrugged, the dark face congealed into a mask.

"I would like to see your engine," said the Brahmard.

"This way, then. It's no different in principle from your airship motor, though: just bigger. Runs off dielectric accumulators. Of course, on a surface ship we have room to carry solar collectors and thus recharge our own system."

"I am surprised that you do not dispense with sails and drive the ship with propellers."

"We do, but only in emergencies. After all, sunlight is not a particularly concentrated energy source. We'd soon exhaust our accumulators if we made them move us at anything like a decent speed. Not even the newest type of fuel cells have capacity enough. As for that indirect form of sunpower storage known as organic fuel . . . well, we have the same problem in the Islands as you do on the continents. Oil, wood, peat, and coal are too expensive for commerical use. But we find the wind quite satisfactory. Except, to be sure, when the engine breaks down and we can't handle our sails! Then I could wish I were on a nice old-fashioned schooner, not this big, proud, thirty-knot tripler.''

''What happened to your engine, anyhow?''

''A freak accident. A defective rotor, operating at high speed, threw a bearing exactly right to break a winding line. I suppose you know that armatures are usually wound with ceramic tubing impregnated with a conductive solution. This in turn shorted out everything else. The damage is reparable. If we'd had ample sea room, we wouldn't have bothered with that SOS.'' Ranu tried to laugh. ''That's why humans are aboard, you know. Theoretically, our computer could be built to do everything. But in practice, something always happens that requires a brain that can think.''

''A computer could be built to do that, too,'' said Dhananda.

''But could it be built to give a damn?'' Ranu muttered in his own language. As he started down a ladder, one of the soldiers came between him and the sun, so that he felt the shadow of a pike across his back.

For centuries after the War of Judgment, the Annaman Islands lay deserted. Their natives regressed easily to a savage state, and took the few outside settlers along. The jungle soon reclaimed those towns the Ingliss had built in their own day. But eventually the outside world recovered somewhat. With its mixed Hinji-Tamil-Paki population firmly under the control of the Udayana Raj, Beneghal accumulated sufficient resources to send out an occasional ship for exploration and trade. A garrison was established on South Annaman. Then the Maurai came. Their more efficient vessels soon dominated seaborne traffic. Nonetheless, Beneghal maintained its claim to the islands. The outpost grew into Port Arberta—which, however, remained small and sleepy, seldom visited by foreign craft.

After the Scientist Revolution in Beneghal put the Brahmards in power, those idealistic oligarchs tried to start an agricultural colony nearby. But the death rate was infamous, and the project was soon discontinued. Since then, as far as the world knew, there had been nothing more important here than a meteorological station.

But the world didn't know much, Ranu reflected.

He and his companions followed the Beneghalis ashore. The wharf lay bare and bleached in the evening light. A few concrete warehouses stood with empty windows. Some primitive fisher boats had obviously lain docked, unused, for months. Beyond the waterfront, palm-thatched huts straggled up from the bay. Ranked trees bespoke a plantation on the other side of the village. Then the jungle began, solid green on the hills, which rose inland in tiers until their ridges gloomed against the purpling east.

How quiet it was! The villagers had come on the run when they sighted the great ship. They stood massed and staring, several hundred of them—native

Annamanese or half-breeds, with black skins and tufty hair and large shy eyes, clad in little more than loincloths. The mainland soldiers towered over them; the Maurai were veritable giants. They should have been swarming about, these people, chattering, shouting, giggling, hustling their wares, the pot-bellied children clamoring for sweets. But they only stared.

Keanua asked bluntly, "What ails these folk? We aren't going to eat them."

"They are afraid of strangers," Dhananda replied. "Slave raiders used to come here."

But that was ended fifty years ago, Ranu thought. *No, any xenophobia they have now is due to rather more recent indoctrination.*

"Besides," the Brahmard went on pointedly, "is it not Maurai doctrine that no culture has the right to meddle with the customs of any other?"

Alisabeta winced. "Yes," she said.

Dhananda made a surface smile. "I am afraid you will find our hospitality somewhat limited here. We haven't many facilities for entertainment."

Ranu looked to his right, past the village, where a steep bluff upheaved itself. On its crest he saw the wooden lattice-work supporting a radio transmitter—chiefly for the use of the weather observers—and some new construction, bungalows and hangars around an airstrip. The earth scars were not entirely healed; this was hardly more than two or three years old. "You seem to be expanding," he remarked with purposeful naïveté.

"Yes, yes," said Dhananda. "Our government still hopes to civilize these islands and open them to

extensive cultivation. Everyone knows that the Beneghali mainland population is bulging at the seams.
But first we must study conditions. Not only the
physical environment which defeated our earlier attempt, but the inland tribes. We want to treat them
fairly; but what does that mean in their own terms?
The old intercultural problem. So we have scientific
teams here, making studies.''

"I see." As she walked toward a waiting donkey
cart, Alisabeta studied the villagers with practical
sympathy. Ranu, who had encountered many odd
folk around the world, believed he could make the
same estimate as she. The little dark people were not
undernourished, although their fishers had not put
out to sea for a long time. They did not watch the
Beneghalis as peasants watch tyrants. Rather, there
was unease in the looks they gave the Maurai.

Water lapped in the bay. A gull mewed, cruising
about with sunlight golden upon its wings. Otherwise the silence grew enormous. It continued after
the donkey trotted off, followed by hundreds of eyes.
When the graveled road came up where the airfield
was, a number of Beneghalis emerged from the
houses to watch. They stood on their verandahs with
the same withdrawn suspiciousness as the islanders.

The stillness was broken by a roar. A man came
bounding down the steps of the largest house and
across the field. He was as tall as Ranu and as broad as
Keanua, dressed in kilt and blouse, his hair and
moustache lurid yellow against a boiled-lobster complexion. A Merican! Ranu stiffened. He saw Alisabeta's fist clench on her knee. Their driver halted the
cart.

"Hoy! Welcome! Dhananda, why in Oktai's name didn't you tell me company was coming?"

The Brahmard looked furious. "We have just gotten here," he answered in a strained voice. "I thought you were—" He broke off.

"At the laboratory for the rest of this week?" the Merican boomed. "Oh yes, so I was, till I heard a foreign ship was approaching the harbor. One of your lads here was talking on the radiophone with our place, asking about our supplies or something. He mentioned it. I overheard. Commandeered an aircraft the first thing. *Why* didn't you let me know? Welcome, you!" He reached a huge paw across the lap of Dhananda, who sat tense, and engulfed Ranu's hand.

"Lorn's the name," he said. "Lorn sunna Browen, of Corado University—and, with all due respect to my good Brahmard colleagues, sick for the sight of a new face. You're Maurai, of course. N'Zealanners, I'd guess. Right?"

He had been a major piece of the jigsaw puzzle that Federation Intelligence had fitted together. Relations between the Sea People and the clans of southwest Merica remained fairly close, however little direct trade went on. After all, missions from Awaii had originally turned those aerial pirates to more peaceable ways. Moreover, despite the slowness and thinness of global communications, an international scientific community did exist. So the Maurai professors had been able to nod confidently and say, yes, that Lorn fellow in Corado is probably the world's leading astrophysicist, and the Brahmards wouldn't hire him for no reason.

But there was nothing furtive about him, Ranu saw. He was genuinely delighted to have visitors.

The Maurai introduced themselves. Lorn jogged alongside the cart, burbling like a cataract. "What, Dhananda, you were going to put them up in that lousy dâk? Nothing doing! I've got my own place here, and plenty of spare room. No, no, Cap'n Ranu, don't bother about thanks. The pleasure is mine. You can show me around your boat if you want to. I'd be interested in that."

"Certainly," said Alisabeta. She gave him her best smile. "Though isn't that a little out of your field?"

Ranu jerked in alarm. But it was Keanua's growl which sounded in their brains: *"Hoai, there, be careful! We're supposed to be plain merchant seamen, remember? We never heard of this Lorn man."*

"I'm sorry!" Her brown eyes widened in dismay. "I forgot."

"Amateurs, the bunch of us," Ranu groaned. *"Let's hope our happy comrade Dhananda is just as inept. But I'm afraid he isn't."*

The Brahmard was watching them keenly. "Why, what do you think the honorable Lorn's work is?" he asked.

"Something to do with your geographical research project," said Alisabeta. "What else?" She cocked her head and pursed her lips. "Now, let me see if I can guess. The Mericans are famous for dry farming . . . but this climate is anything except dry. They are also especially good at mining and ore processing. Ah, hah! You've found heavy-metal deposits in the jungle and aren't letting on."

Lorn, who had grown embarrassed under Dhananda's glare, cleared his throat and said with false heartiness: "Well, now, we don't want news to get around too fast, you understand? Spring a surprise on the mercantile world, eh?"

"Best leave the explanations to me, honorable sir." Dhananda's words fell like lumps of stone. The two soldiers accompanying the party in the cart hefted their scabbarded swords. Lorn glowered and clapped a hand to his broad clansman's dagger.

The moment passed. The cart stopped before a long white bungalow. Servants—mainlanders who walked like men better accustomed to uniforms than livery—took the guests' baggage and bowed them in. They were given adjoining bedrooms, comfortably furnished in the ornate upper-class Hinji style. Since he knew his stuff would be searched anyway, Ranu let a valet help him change into a formal shirt and sarong. But he kept his knife. That was against modern custom, when bandits and barbarians were no longer quite so likely to come down the chimney. Nonetheless, Ranu was not going to let this knife out of his possession.

The short tropic twilight was upon them when they gathered on the verandah for drinks. Dhananda sat in a corner, nursing a glass of something nonalcoholic. Ranu supposed the Brahmard—obviously the security chief here—had pulled rank on Lorn and insisted on being invited to eat. The Maurai skipper stretched out in a wicker chair with Keanua on his left, Alisabeta on his right, Lorn confronting them.

Darkness closed in, deep and blue. The sea glimmered below; the land lay black, humping up toward stars that one by one trod brilliantly forth. Yellow candlelight spilled from windows where the dinner table was being set. Bats darted on the fringe of sight. A lizard scuttled in the thatch overhead. From the jungle came sounds of wild pigs grunting, the scream of a startled peacock, numberless insect chirps. Coolness descended layer by layer, scented with jasmine.

Lorn mopped his brow and cheeks. "I wish to God I were back in Corado," he said in his own Ingliss-descended language, which he was gladdened to hear Ranu understood. "This weather gets me. My clan has a lodge on the north rim of the Grand Canyon. Pines and deer and— Oh, well, it's worth a couple of years here. Not just the pay." Briefly, something like holiness touched the heavy features. "The work."

"I beg your pardon," Dhananda interrupted from the shadows, "but no one else knows what you are telling us."

"Oh, sorry. I forgot." The Merican switched to his badly accented Hinji. "I wanted to say, friends, when I finish here I'd like to go home via N'Zealann. It must be about the most interesting place on Earth. Wellantoa's damn near the capital of the planet, or will be one day, eh?"

"Perhaps!" Dhananda snapped.

"No offense," said Lorn. "I don't belong to the Sea People either, you know. But they are the most progressive country going."

"In certain ways," Dhananda conceded. "In others—forgive me, guests, if I call your policies a little antiprogressive. For example, your consistent discouragement of attempts to civilize the world's barbarian societies."

"Not that exactly," defended Ranu. "When they offer a clear threat to their neighbors, of course the Federation is among the first powers to send in the peace enforcers—which, in the long run, means psychodynamic teams, to redirect the energies of the barbarians concerned. A large-scale effort is being mounted at this moment in Sina, as I'm sure you have heard."

"Just like you did with my ancestors, eh?" said Lorn, unabashed.

"Well, yes. But the point is, we don't want to mold anyone else into our own image; nor see them molded into the image of, say, Beneghali factory workers or Meycan peons or Orgonian foresters. So our government does exert pressure on other civilized governments to leave the institutions of backward peoples as much alone as possible."

"Why?" Dhananda leaned forward. His beard jutted aggressively. "It's easy enough for you Maurai. Your population growth is under control. You have your sea ranches, your synthetics plants, your world-wide commerce. Do you think the rest of mankind is better off in poverty, slavery, and ignorance?"

"Of course not," said Alisabeta. "But they'll get over that by themselves, in their own ways. Our trade and our example—I mean all the more advanced countries—such things can help. But they mustn't help too much, or the same thing will happen again that happened before the War of Judgment. I mean . . . what's the Hinji word? We call it cultural pseudomorphosis."

"A mighty long word for a lady as cute as you," said Lorn sunna Browen. He sipped his gin noisily, leaned over and patted her knee. Ranu gathered that his family had stayed behind when the Brahmards hired him for this job; and in their primness they had not furnished him with a surrogate.

"You know," the Merican went on, "I'm surprised that merchant seamen can talk as academically as you do."

"Not me," grinned Keanua. "I'm strictly a deck-hand type."

"I notice you have a bamboo flute tucked in your sarong," Lorn pointed out.

"Well, uh, I do play a little. To while away the watches."

"Indeed," murmured Dhananda. "And your conversation is very well informed, Captain Makin-tairu."

"Why shouldn't it be?" answered the Maurai, surprised. He thought of the irony if they should suspect he was not really a tramp-ship skipper. Because he was nothing else; he had been nothing else his whole adult life. "I went to school," he said. "We take books along on our voyages. We talk with people in foreign ports. That's all."

"Nevertheless—" Dhananda paused. "It is true," he admitted reflectively, "that Federation citizens in general have the reputation of being rather intellectual. More, even, than would be accounted for by your admirable hundred-percent literacy rate."

"Oh no." Alisabeta laughed. "I assure you, we're the least scholarly race alive. We like to learn, of course, and think and argue. But isn't that simply one of the pleasures in life, among many others? Our technology does give us abundant leisure for that sort of thing."

"Ours doesn't," said Dhananda grimly.

"Too many people, too few resources," Lorn agreed. "You must've been to Calcut before, m' lady. But have you ever seen the slums? And I'll bet you never traveled through the hinterland and watched those poor dusty devils trying to scratch a living from the agrocollectives."

"I did once," said Keanua with compassion.

"Well!" Lorn shook himself, tossed off his drink, and rose. "We've gotten far too serious. I assure you, m' lady, we aren't dry types at Corado University either. I'd like to take you and a couple of crossbows with me into the Rockies after mountain goat . . . Come, I hear the dinner gong." He took Alisabeta's arm.

Ranu trailed after. *Mustn't overeat,* he thought. *This night looks like the best time to start prowling.*

There was no moon. The time for the *Aorangi* had been chosen with that in mind. Ranu woke at midnight, as he had told himself to do. He had the common Maurai knack of sleeping a short time and being refreshed thereby. Sliding off the bed, he stood for minutes looking out and listening. The airstrip reached bare beyond the house, gray under the stars. The windows in one hangar showed light.

A sentry tramped past. His forest-green turban and clothes, his dark face, made him another blackness. But a sheen went along his gun barrel. An actual explosive-cartridge rifle. And . . . his beat took him by this house.

Still, he was only one man. He should have been

given partners. The Brahmards were as unskilled in secrecy and espionage as the Maurai. When Earth held a mere four or five scientifically-minded nations, with scant and slow traffic between them, serious conflict rarely arose. Even today Beneghal did not maintain a large army. Larger than the Federation's —but Beneghal was a land power and needed protection against barbarians. The Maurai had a near monopoly on naval strength, for a corresponding reason; and it wasn't much of a navy.

Call them, with truth, as horrible as you liked, those centuries during which the human race struggled back from the aftermath of nuclear war had had an innocence that the generations before the Judgment lacked. *I am afraid*, thought Ranu with a sadness that surprised him a bit, *we too are about to lose that particular virginity.*

No time for sentiment. *"Keanua, Alisabeta,"* he called in his head. He felt them come to alertness. *"I'm going out for a look."*

"Is that wise?" The girl's worry fluttered in him. *"If you should be caught—"*

"My chances are best now. We have them off-balance, arriving so unexpectedly. But I bet Dhananda will double his precautions tomorrow, after he's worried overnight that we might be spies."

"Be careful, then," Keanua said. Ranu felt a kinesthetic overtone, as if a hand reached under the pillow for a knife. *"Yell if you run into trouble. I think we might fight our way clear."*

"Oh! Stay away from the front entrance," Alisabeta warned. *"When Lorn took me out on the verandah after dinner to talk, I noticed a man squat-*

ting under the willow tree there. He may just have been an old syce catching a breath of air, but more likely he's an extra watchman.''

''Thanks.'' Ranu omitted any flowery Maurai leave-taking. His friends would be in contact. But he felt their feelings like a handclasp about him. Neither had questioned that he must be the one who ventured forth. As captain, he had the honor and obligation to assume extra hazards. Yet Keanua grumbled and fretted, and there was something in the girl's mind, less a statement than a color: she felt closer to him than to any other man.

Briefly, he wished for the physical touch of her. But— The guard was safely past. Ranu glided out the open window.

For a space he lay flat on the verandah. Faint stirrings and voices came to him from the occupied hangar. Candles had been lit in one bungalow. The rest slept, ghostly under the sky. So far nothing was happening in the open. Ranu slithered down into the flowerbed. Too late he discovered it included roses. He bit back a sailor's oath and crouched for minutes more.

All right, better get started. He had no special training in sneakery, but most Maurai learned judo arts in school, and afterward their work and their sports kept them supple. He went like a shadow among shadows, rounding the field until he came to one of the new storehouses.

Covered by the gloom at a small rear door, he drew his knife. A great deal of miniaturized circuitry had been packed into its handle, together with a tiny accumulator cell. The jewel on the pommel was a lens, and when he touched it in the right way a pencil beam of blue light sprang forth. He examined the lock. Not plastic, nor even aluminum bronze: steel. And the door was iron reinforced. What was so valuable inside?

From Ranu's viewpoint, a ferrous lock was a lucky break. He turned the knife's inconspicuous controls probing and grasping with magnetic pulses, resolutely suppressing the notion that every star was staring at him. After a long and sweaty while, he heard tumblers click. He opened the door gently and went through.

His beam flickered about. The interior held mostly shelves, from floor to ceiling, loaded with paperboard cartons. He padded across the room, chose a box on a rear shelf that wouldn't likely be noticed for weeks, and slit the tape. Hm . . . as expected. A dielectric energy accumulator, molecular-distortion type. Standard equipment, employed by half the powered engines in the world.

But so many—in this outpost of loneliness?

His sample was fresh, too. Uncharged. Maurai agents had already seen, from commercial aircraft that "happened" to be blown off course, that there was only one solar-energy collection station on the whole archipelago. Nor did the islands have hydroelectric or tidal generators. Yet obviously these cells had been shipped here to be charged.

Which meant that the thing in the hills had developed much further than Federation Intelligence knew.

"Nan damn it," Ranu whispered. "Shark-toothed Nan damn and devour it."

He stood for a little turning the black cube over and over in his hands. His skin prickled. Then, with a shiver, he repacked the cell and left the storehouse as quietly as he had entered.

Outside he paused. Ought he to do anything else? This one bit of information justified the whole *Aorangi* enterprise. If he tried for more and failed, and his coworkers died with him, the effort would have gone for nothing.

However . . . . Time was hideously short. An alarmed Dhananda would find ways to keep other foreigners off the island—a faked wreck or something to make the harbor unusable—until too late. At least, Ranu must assume so.

He did not agonize over his decision; that was not a Maurai habit. He made it. *Let's have a peek in that lighted hangar, just for luck, before going to bed. Tomorrow I'll try and think of some way to get inland and see the laboratory.*

A cautious half hour later, he stood flattened against a wall and peered through a window. The vaulted interior of the hangar was nearly filled by a pumped-up gasbag. Motors idled, hardly audible, propellers not yet engaged. Several mechanics were making final checks. Two men from the bungalow where candles had been lit—Brahmards themselves, to judge from their white garb and authoritative manner—stood waiting while some junior attendants loaded boxed apparatus into the gondola. Above the whirr, Ranu caught a snatch of talk between them:

"—unsanctified hour. Why *now*, for Vishnu's sake?"

"These fool newcomers. They might not be distressed mariners, ever think of that? In any case, they mustn't see us handling stuff like this.'' Four men staggered past bearing a coiled cable. The uninsulated ends shone the red of pure copper. "You don't use that for geographical research, what?"

Ranu felt his hair stir.

Two soldiers embarked with guns. Ranu doubted they were going along merely because of the monetary value of that cable, fabulous though it was.

The scientists followed. The ground crew manned a capstan. Their ancient, wailing chant came like a protest—that human muscles must go strain when a hundred horses snored in the same room. The hangar roof and front wall folded creakily aside.

Ranu went rigid.

He must unconsciously have shot his thought to the other Maurai. *"No!"* Alisabeta cried to him.

Keanua said more slowly: *"That's cannibal recklessness, skipper. You might fall and smear yourself over three degrees of latitude. Or if you should be seen—"*

"I'll never have a better chance," Ranu said. *"We've already invented a dozen different cover stories in case I disappear. So pick one and use it."*

"But you," Alisabeta begged. *"Alone out there!"*

"It might be worse for you, if Dhananda should decide to get tough," Ranu answered. The Ingliss single-mindedness had come upon him, overriding the easy, indolent Maurai blood. But then that second heritage woke with a shout, for those who first possessed N'Zealann, the canoe men and moa hunters, would have dived laughing into an escapade like this.

He pushed down the glee and related what he had

found in the storehouse. *"If you feel any doubt about your own safety, any time, forget me and leave,"* he ordered. *"Intelligence has got to know at least this much. If I'm detected yonder in the hills, I'll try to get away and hide in the jungle."* The hangar was open, the aircraft slipping its cables, the propellers becoming bright transparent circles as they were engaged. *"Farewell. Good luck."*

"Tanaroa be with you," Alisabeta called through her tears.

Ranu dashed around the corner. The aircraft rose on a slant, gondola an ebony slab, bag a pale storm cloud. The propellers threw wind in his face. He ran along the vessel's shadow, poised, and sprang.

Almost, he didn't make it. His fingers closed on something, slipped, clamped with the strength of terror. Both hands, now! He was gripping an iron-wood bar, part of the mooring gear, his legs atangle over an earth that fell away below him with appalling swiftness. He sucked in a breath and chinned himself, got one knee over the bar, clung there and gasped.

The electric motors purred. A breeze whittered among struts and spars. Otherwise Ranu was alone with his heartbeat. After a while it slowed. He hitched himself to a slightly more comfortable crouch and looked about. The jungle was black, dappled with dark gray, far underneath him. The sea that edged it shimmered in starlight with exactly the same whiteness as the nacelles along the gondola. He heard a friendly creaking of wickerwork, felt a sort of throb as the gasbag expanded in this higher-level air. The constellations wheeled grandly around him.

He had read about jet aircraft that outpaced the sun, before the nuclear war. Once he had seen a representation, on a fragment of ancient cinema film discovered by archeologists and transferred to new acetate; a sound track had been included. He did not understand how anyone could want to sit locked in a howling coffin like that when he might have swum through the air, intimate with the night sky, as Ranu was now doing.

However precariously, his mind added with wryness. He had not been seen, and he probably wasn't affecting the trim enough to make the pilot suspicious. Nevertheless, he had scant time to admire the view. The bar along which he sprawled, the sisal guy on which he leaned one shoulder, dug into his flesh. His muscles were already tiring. If this trip was any slower than he had guessed it would be, he'd tumble to earth.

Or else be too clumsy to spring off unseen and melt into darkness as the aircraft landed.

Or when he turned up missing in the morning, Dhananda might guess the truth and lay a trap for him.

Or anything! Stop your fuss, you idiot. You need all your energy for hanging on.

The Brahmard's tread was light on the verandah, but Alisabeta's nerves were strung so taut that she sensed him and turned about with a small gasp. For a second they regarded each other, unspeaking, the dark, slight, bearded man in his neat whites and the strongly built girl whose skin seemed to glow golden in the shade of a trellised grapevine. Beyond, the airstrip flimmered in midmorning sunlight. Heat hazes wavered on the hangar roofs.

"You have not found him?" she asked at last, without tone.

Dhananda's head shook slowly, as if his turban had become heavy. "No. Not a trace. I came back to ask you if you have any idea where he might have gone."

"I told your deputy my guess. Ranu . . . Captain Makintairu is in the habit of taking a swim before breakfast. He may have gone down to the shore about dawn and—" She hoped he would take her hesitation to mean no more than an unspoken: *Sharks. Rip tides. Cramp.*

But the sable gaze continued to probe her. "It is most improbable that he could have left this area unobserved," Dhananda said. "You have seen our guards. More of them are posted downhill."

"What are you guarding against?" she counterattacked, to divert him. "Are you less popular with the natives than you claim to be?"

He parried her almost contemptuously: "We have reason to think two of the Buruman pirate kings have made alliance and gotten some aircraft. We do have equipment and materials here that would be worth stealing. Now, about Captain Makintairu. I cannot believe he left unseen unless he did so deliberately, taking great trouble about it. Why?"

"I don't know, I tell you!"

"You must admit we are duty bound to consider the possibility that you are not simple merchant mariners."

"What else? Pirates ourselves? Don't be absurd."
I dare you to accuse us of being spies. Because then I
will ask what there is here to spy on.

Only . . .then what will you do?

Dhananda struck the porch railing with a fist.
Bitterness spoke: "Your Federation swears so piously
it doesn't intervene in the development of other cultures."

"Except when self-defense forces us to," Alisabeta
said. "And only a minimum."

He ignored that. "In the name of noninter-
vention, you are always prepared to refuse some
country the sea-ranching equipment that would give
it a new start, or bribe somebody else *with* such
equipment not to begin a full-fledged merchant
service to a third and backward country . . . a service
that might bring the backward country up-to-date in
less than a generation. You talk about encouraging
cultural diversity. You seem seriously to believe it's
moral keeping the Okkaidans impoverished fisher-
men so they'll be satisfied to write haiku and grow
dwarf gardens for recreation. And yet—by Kali herself, your agents are everywhere!"

"If you don't want us here," Alisabeta snapped,
"deport us and complain to our government."

"I may have to do more than that."

"But I swear—"

"Alisabeta! Keanua!"

Distance-attenuated, Ranu's message still stiffened
her where she stood. She felt his tension, and an
undertone of hunger and thirst, like a thrum along
her own nerves. The verandah faded about her, and
she stood in murk and heard a slamming of great
pumps. Was there really a red warning light that

went flash-flash-flash above a bank of transformers taller than a man?

"*Yes, I'm inside,*" the rapid, blurred voice said in her skull. "*I watched my chance from the jungle edge. When an oxcart came along the trail with a sleepy native driver, I clung to the bottom and was carried through the gates. Food supplies. Evidently the workers here have a contract with some nearby village. The savages bring food and do guard duty. I've seen at least three of them prowling about with blowguns. Anyhow, I'm in. I dropped from the cart and slipped into a side tunnel. Now I'm sneaking around, hoping not to be seen.*

"*The place is huge! They must have spent years enlarging a chain of natural caves. Air conduits everywhere—I daresay that's how our signals are getting through; I sense you, but faintly. Forced ventilation, with thermostatic controls. Can you imagine power expenditure on such a scale? I'm going toward the center of things now for a look. My signal will probably be screened out till I come back near the entrance again.*"

"*Don't, skipper,*" Keanua pleaded. "*You've seen plenty. We know for a fact that Intelligence guessed right. That's enough.*"

"*Not quite,*" Ranu said. The Maurai rashness flickered along the edge of his words. "*I want to see if the project is as far advanced as I fear. If not, perhaps the Federation won't have to take emergency measures. I'm afraid we will, though.*"

"*Ranu!*" Alisabeta called. His thought enfolded her. But static exploded, interfering energies that hurt her perceptions. When it lifted, an emptiness was in her head where Ranu had been.

"Are you ill, my lady?" Dhananda barked the question.

She looked dazedly out at the sky, unable to answer. He moved nearer. "What are you doing?" he pressed.

"*Steady, girl,*" Keanua rumbled.

Alisabeta swallowed, squared her shoulders, and faced the Brahmard. "I'm worrying about Captain Makintairu," she said coldly. "Does that satisfy you?"

"No."

"Hoy, there, you!" rang a voice from the front door. Lorn sunna Browen came forth. His kilted form overtopped them both; the light eyes sparked at Dhananda. "What kind of hospitality is this? Is he bothering you, my lady?"

"I am not certain that these people have met the obligations of guests," Dhananda said, his control cracking open.

Lorn put arms akimbo, fists knotted. "Until you can prove that, though, just watch your manners. Eh? As long as I'm here, this is my house, not yours."

"Please," Alisabeta said. She hated fights. Why had she ever volunteered for this job? "I beg you . . . don't."

Dhananda made a jerky bow. "Perhaps I am over-zealous," he said without conviction. "If so, I ask your pardon. I shall continue the search for the captain."

"I think—meanwhile—I'll go down to our ship and help Keanua with the repairs," Alisabeta whispered.

"Very well," said Dhananda.

Lorn took her arm. "Mind if I come too? You, uh, you might like to have a little distraction from thinking about your poor friend. And I never have seen an oceangoing craft close by. They flew me here when I was hired."

"I suggest you return to your own work, sir," Dhananda said in a harsh tone.

"When I'm good and ready, I will," Lorn answered airily. "Come, Miss . . . uh . . . m'lady." He led Alisabeta down the stair and around the strip. Dhananda watched from the portico, motionless.

"You mustn't mind him," Lorn said after a bit. "He's not a bad sort. A nice family man, in fact, pretty good chess player, and a devil on the polo field. But this has been a long grind, and his responsibility has kind of worn him down."

"Oh yes. I understand," Alisabeta said. *But still he frightens me.*

Lorn ran a hand through his thinning yellow mane. "Most Brahmards are pretty decent," he said. "I've come to know them in the time I've been working here. They're recruited young, you know, with psychological tests to weed out those who don't have the . . . the dedication, I guess you'd call it. Oh, sure, naturally they enjoy being a boss caste. But somebody has to be. No Hinjan country has the resources or the elbow room to govern itself as loosely as you Sea People do. The Brahmards want to modernize Beneghal—eventually the world. Get mankind back where it was before the War of Judgment, and go on from there."

"I know," Alisabeta said.

"I don't see why you Maurai are so dead set against that. Don't you realize how many people go to bed hungry every night?"

"Of course, of course we do!" she burst out. It angered her that tears should come so close to the surface of her eyes. "But so they did before the War. Can't anyone else see . . . turning the planet into one huge factory isn't the answer? Have you read any history? Did you ever hear of . . . oh, just to name one movement that called itself progressive . . . the Communists? They too were going to end poverty and famine. They were going to reorganize society along rational lines. Well, we have contemporary records to prove that in Rossaya alone, in the first thirty or forty years it had power, their regime killed twenty million of their own citizens. Starved them, shot them, worked them to death in labor camps. The total deaths, in all the Communist countries, may have gone as high as a hundred million. And this was *before* evangelistic foreign policies brought on nuclear war. How many famines and plagues would it take to wipe out that many human lives? And how much was the life of the survivors worth, under such masters?"

"But the Brahmards aren't like that," he protested. "See for yourself, down in this village. The natives are well taken care of. Nobody abuses them or coerces them. Same thing on the mainland. There's a lot of misery yet in Beneghal—mass starvation going on right now—but it'll be overcome."

"Why haven't the villagers been fishing?" she challenged.

"Eh?" Taken aback, Lorn paused on the downhill

path. The sun poured white across them both, made the bay a bowl of molten brass, and seemed to flatten the jungle leafage into one solid listless green. The air was very empty and quiet. But Ranu crept through the belly of a mountain, where machines hammered . . . .

"Well, it hasn't been practical to allow that," said the Merican. "Some of our work is confidential. We can't risk information leaking out. But the Beneghalis have been feeding them. Oktai, it amounts to a holiday for the fishers. They aren't complaining."

Alisabeta decided to change the subject, or even this big bundle of guilelessness might grow suspicious. "So you're a scientist," she said. "How interesting. But what do they need you here for? I mean, they have good scientists of their own."

"I . . . uh . . . I have specialized knowledge which is, uh, applicable," he said. "You know how the sciences and technologies hang together. Your Island biotechs breed new species to concentrate particular metals out of seawater, so naturally they need metallurgic data too. In my own case—uh—" Hastily: "I do want to visit your big observatory in N'Zealann on my way home. I hear they've photographed an ancient artificial satellite, still circling the Earth after all these centuries. I think maybe some of the records our archeologists have dug up in Merica would enable us to identify it. Knowing its original orbit and so forth, we could compute out a lot of information about the solar system."

"Tanaroa, yes!" Despite everything, eagerness jumped in her.

His red face, gleaming with sweat, lifted toward

the blank blue sky. "Of course," he murmured, almost to himself, "that's a piddle compared to what we'd learn if we could get back out there in person."

"Build space probes again? Or actual manned ships?"

"Yes. If we had the power, and the industrial plant. By Oktai, but I get sick of this!" Lorn exclaimed. His grip on her arm tightened unconsciously until she winced. "Scraping along on lean ores, tailings, scrap, synthetics, substitutes . . . because the ancients exhausted so much. Exhausted the good mines, most of the fossil fuels, coal, petroleum, uranium. . . then smashed their industry in the War and let the machines corrode away to unrecoverable dust in the dark ages that followed. That's what's holding us back, girl. We know everything our ancestors did and then some. But we haven't got the equipment they had to process materials on the scale they did, and we haven't the natural resources to rebuild that equipment. A vicious circle. We haven't got the capital to make it economically feasible to produce the giant industries that could accumulate the capital."

"I think we're doing quite well," she said, gently disengaging herself. "Sunpower, fuel cells, wind and water, biotechnology, sea ranches and sea farms, efficient agriculture—"

"We could do better, though." His arm swept a violent arc that ended with a finger pointed at the bay. "There! The oceans. Every element in the periodic table is dissolved in them. Billions of tons. But we'll never get more than a minimum out with your fool solar and biological methods. We need energy. Power to evaporate water by the cubic kilometer. Power to synthesize oil by the megabarrel. Power to go to the stars.''

The rapture faded. He seemed shaken by his own words, shut his lips as if retreating behind the walrus moustache, and resumed walking. Alisabeta came along in silence. Their feet scrunched in gravel and sent up little puffs of dust. Presently the dock resounded under them; they boarded the *Aorangi*, and went across to the engine-room hatch.

Keanua paused in his labors as they entered. He had opened the aluminum-alloy casing and spread parts out on the deck, where he squatted in a sunbeam from an open porthole. Elsewhere the room was cool and shadowy; wavelets lapped the hull.

"Good day," said the Taiitian. His smile was perfunctory, his thoughts inside the mountain with Ranu.

"Looks as if you're immobilized for a while," Lorn said, lounging back against a flame-grained bulkhead panel.

"Until we find what has happened to our friend, surely," Keanua answered.

"I'm sorry about him," Lorn said. "I hope he comes back soon."

"Well, we can't wait indefinitely for him," Alisabeta made herself say. "If he isn't found by the time the engine is fixed, best we start for Calcut. Your group will send him on when he does appear, won't you?"

"Sure," said Lorn. "If he's alive. Uh, 'scuse me, my lady."

"No offense. We don't hold with euphemisms in the Islands."

"It does puzzle the deuce out of me," Keanua grunted. "He's a good swimmer, if he did go for a swim. Of course, he might have taken a walk instead, into the jungle. Are you sure the native tribes are always peaceful?"

"Um—"

"Can you hear me? Can you hear me?"

Ranu's voice was as tiny in Alisabeta's head as the scream of an insect. But they felt the pain that jagged in it. He had been wounded.

"Get out! Get away as fast as you can! I've seen— the thing—it's working! I swear it must be working. Pouring out power . . . some kind of chemosynthetic plant beyond— They saw me as I started back. Put a blowgun dart in my thigh. Alarms hooting everywhere. I think I can beat them to the entrance, though, get into the forest—"

Keanua had leaped to his feet. The muscles moved like snakes under his skin. *"Escape, with natives tracking you?"* he snarled.

Ranu's signal strengthened as he came nearer the open air. *"This place has radiophone contact with the town. Dhananda's undoubtedly being notified right now. Get clear, you two!"*

"If . . . if we can," Alisabeta faltered. *"But you—"*

"GET UNDER WEIGH, I TELL YOU!"

Lorn stared from one to another of them. "What's wrong?" A hand dropped to his knife. Years at a desk had not much slowed his mountaineer's reflexes.

Alisabeta glanced past him at Keanua. There was no need for words. The Taiitian's grasp closed on Lorn's dagger wrist.

"What the hell—!" The Merican yanked with skill. His arm snapped out between the thumb and fingers holding him, and a sunbeam flared off steel.

Keanua closed in. His left arm batted sideways to deflect the knife. His right hand, stiffly held, poked at the solar plexus. But Lorn's left palm came chopping down, edge on. A less burly wrist than Keanua's would have broken. As it was, the sailor choked on an oath and went pale around the nostrils. Lorn snatched his opponent's knife from the sheath and threw it out the porthole.

The Merican could then have ripped Keanua's belly. But instead he paused. "What's got into you?" he asked in a high, bewildered voice. "Miss Alisa—" He half looked around for her.

Keanua recovered enough to go after the clansman's dagger. One arm under the wrist for a fulcrum, the other arm applying the leverage of his whole body—Lorn's hand bent down, the fingers were pulled open by their own tendons, the blade tinkled to the deck. "Get it, girl!" Keanua said. He kicked it aside. Lorn had already grappled him.

Alisabeta slipped past their trampling legs to snatch the weapon. Her pulse thuttered in her throat. It was infinitely horrible that the sun should pour so brilliant through the porthole. The chuckle of water on the hull was lost in the rough breath and stamp of feet, back and forth as the fight swayed. Lorn struck with a poleax fist, but Keanua dropped his head and took the blow on his skull. Anguish stabbed through the Merican's knuckles. He let go his adversary. Keanua followed the advantage, seeking a stranglehold. Lorn's foot lashed out, caught the Taiitian in the stomach, sent him lurching away.

No time to gape! Alisabeta ran up the ladder onto the main deck. A few black children stood on the wharf, sucking their thumbs and staring endlessly at the ship. Except for them, Port Arberta seemed asleep. But no, yonder in the heat shimmer . . . dust on the downhill path . . . . She shaded her eyes. A man in white and three soldiers in green; headed this way, surely. Dhananda had been informed that a spy had entered the secret place. Now he was on his way to arrest the spy's indubitable accomplices.

But with only three men?

Wait! He doesn't know about head-to-head. He can't tell that we here know he knows about Ranu. So he plans to capture us by surprise—so we won't destroy evidence or scuttle the ship or something— Yes, he'll come aboard with some story about searching for Ranu, and have his men aim their guns at us when he makes a signal. Not before.

"*Ranu, what should I do?*"

There was no answer, only—when she concentrated—a sense of pain in the muscles, fire in the lungs, heat and sweat and running. He fled through the jungle with the blowgun men on his trail, unable to think of anything but a hiding place.

Alisabeta bit her nails. Lesu Haristi, Son of Tanaroa, what to do, what to do? She had been about to call the advance base on Car Nicbar. A single radio shout, to tell them what had been learned, and then surrender to Dhananda. But that was a desperation measure. It would openly involve the Federation government. Worse, any outsider who happened to be tuned to that band—and considerable radio talk went on these days—might well record and decode and get some inkling of what was here and tell the world. And this would in time start similar kettles boiling elsewhere . . . and the Federation couldn't sit on that many lids, didn't want to, wasn't equipped to— *Stop maundering, you ninny! Make up your mind!*

Alisabeta darted back down into the engine room. Keanua and Lorn rolled on the deck, locked together. She picked a wrench from among the tools and poised it above the Merican's head. His scalp shone pinkly through the yellow hair, a bald spot, and last night he had shown her pictures of his children . . . . No. She couldn't. She threw the wrench aside, pulled off her lap-lap, folded it into a strip, and drew it carefully around Lorn's throat. A twist; he choked and released Keanua; the Taiitian got a grip and throttled him unconscious in thirty seconds.

"Thanks! Don't know . . . if I could have done that . . . alone. Strong's an orca, him." As he talked Keanua deftly bound and gagged the Merican. Lorn stirred, blinked, writhed helplessly, and glared his hurt and anger.

Alisabeta had already slid back a certain panel. The compartment behind held the other engine, the one that was not damaged. She connected it to the gears while she told Keanua what she had seen. "If we work it right, I think we can also capture those other men," she said. "That'll cause confusion, and they'll be useful hostages, am I right?"

"Right. Good girl." Keanua slapped her bottom and grinned. Remembering Beneghali customs, she put the lap-lap on again and went topside.

Dhananda and his guards reached the dock a few minutes later. She waved at them but kept her place by the saloon cabin door. They crossed the gangplank, which boomed under their boots. The Brahmard's countenance was stormy. "Where are the others?" he demanded.

"In there." She nodded at the cabin. "Having a drink. Won't you join us?"

He hesitated. "If you will too, my lady."

"Of course." She went ahead. The room was long, low, and cool, furnished with little more than straw mats and shoji screens. Keanua stepped from behind one of them. He held a repeating blowgun.

"Stay where you are, friends," he ordered around the mouthpiece. "Raise your hands."

A soldier spat a curse and snatched for his submachine gun. Keanua puffed. The feeder mechanism clicked. Three darts buried themselves in the planking at the soldier's feet. "Cyanide," Keanua reminded them. He kept the bamboo tube steady. "Next time I aim to kill."

"What do you think you are doing?" Dhananda breathed. His features had turned almost gray. But he lifted his arms with the others. Alisabeta took their weapons. She cast the guns into a corner as if they were hot to the touch.

"Secure them," Keanua said. He made the prisoners lie down while the girl hogtied them. Afterward he carried each below through a hatch in the saloon deck to a locker where Lorn already lay. As he made Dhananda fast to a shackle bolt he said, "We're going to make a break for it. Would you like to tell your men ashore to let us go without a fight? I'll run a microphone down here for you."

"No," Dhananda said. "You pirate swine."

"Suit yourself. But if we get sunk you'll drown too. Think about that." Keanua went back topside.

Alisabeta stood by the cabin door, straining into a silence that hissed. "I can't hear him at all," she said from the verge of tears. "Is he dead?"

"No time for that now," Keanua said. "We've got to get started. Take the wheel. I think once we're past the headland, we'll pick up a little wind."

She nodded dumbly and went to the pilothouse. Keanua cast off. Several adult villagers materialized as if by sorcery to watch. The engine pulsed, screws caught the water, the *Aorangi* stood out into the bay. Keanua moved briskly about, preparing the ship's armament. It was standard for a civilian vessel: a catapult throwing bombs of jellied fish oil, two flywheel guns that cast streams of small sharp rocks. Since pirates couldn't get gunpowder, merchantmen saw no reason to pay its staggering cost. One of the Intelligence officers had wanted to supply a rocket launcher, but Ranu had pointed out that it would be hard enough to conceal the extra engine.

Men must be swarming like ants on the hilltop. Alisabeta watched four of them come down on horseback. The dust smoked behind them. They flung open the doors of a boathouse and emerged in a watercraft that zoomed within hailing distance.

A Beneghali officer rose in the stern sheets and bawled through a megaphone—his voice was soon lost on that sun-dazzled expanse—"Ahoy, there! Where are you bound?"

"Your chief's commandeered us to make a search," Keanua shouted back.

"Yes? Where is he? Let me speak to him."

"He's below. Can't come now."

"Stand by to be boarded."

Keanua said rude things. Alisabeta guided the ship out through the channel, scarcely hearing. Partly she was fighting down a sense of sadness and defilement—she had attacked guests—and partly she kept crying for Ranu to answer. Only the gulls did.

The boat darted back to shore. Keanua came aft. "They'll be at us before long," he said bleakly. "I told 'em their own folk would go down with us, and they'd better negotiate instead. Implying we really are pirates, you know. But they wouldn't listen."

"Certainly not," Alisabeta said. "Every hour of haggling is time gained for us. They know that."

Keanua sighed. "Well, so it goes. I'll holler to Nicbar."

"What signal?" Though cipher messages would be too risky, a few codes had been agreed upon: mere standardized impulses, covering preset situations.

"Attack. Come here as fast as they can with everything they've got," Keanua decided.

"Just to save our lives? Oh no!"

The Taiitian shook his head. "To wipe out that damned project in the hills. Else the Brahmards will get the idea, and mount so big a guard from now on that we won't be able to come near without a full-scale war."

He stood quiet awhile. "Two of us on this ship,

and a couple hundred of them," he said. "We'll have a tough time staying alive, girl, till the relief expedition gets close enough for a head-to-head." He yawned and stretched, trying to ease his tension. "Of course, I'd rather like to stay alive for my own sake, too."

There was indeed a breeze on the open sea, which freshened slightly as the *Aorangi* moved south. They set the computer to direct sail hoisting and disengaged the screws. The engine would be required at full capacity to power the weapons. After putting the wheel on autopilot, Keanua and Alisabeta helped each other into quilted combat armor and alloy helmets.

Presently the airships came aloft. That was the sole possible form of onslaught, she knew. With their inland mentalities, the Brahmards had stationed no naval units here. There were—one, two, three—a full dozen vessels, big and bright in the sky. They assumed formation and lined out in pursuit.

Ranu awoke so fast that for a moment he blinked about him in wonderment: where was he, what had happened? He lay in a hollow beneath a fallen tree, hidden by a cascade of trumpet-flower vines. The sun turned their leaves nearly yellow; the light here behind them was thick and green, the air unspeakably hot. He couldn't be sure how much of the crawling over his body was sweat and how much was ants. His right thigh needled him where the dart had pierced it. A smell of earth and crushed vegetation filled his nostrils, mingled with his own stench. Nothing but his heartbeat and the distant liquid notes of a bulbul interrupted noonday silence.

Oh yes, he recalled wearily. *I got out the main entrance. Stiff-armed a sentry and sprang into the brush. A score of Beneghalis after me . . . shook them, but just plain had to outrun the natives . . . longer legs. I hope I covered my trail, once beyond their sight. Must have, or they'd've found me here by now. I've been unconscious for hours.*

The ship!

Remembrance rammed into him. He sucked a breath between his teeth, nearly jumped from his hiding place, recovered his wits and dug fingers into the mold under his belly. At last he felt able to reach forth head-to-head.

"Alisabeta! Are you there? Can you hear me?"

Her answer was instant. Not words—a gasp, a laugh, a sob, clearer and stronger than he had ever known before; and as their minds embraced, some deeper aspect of self. Suddenly he became her, aboard the ship.

No more land was to be seen, only the ocean, blue close at hand, shining like mica farther out where the sun smote it. The wreckage of an aircraft bobbed a kilometer to starboard, gondola projecting from beneath the flattened bag. The other vessels maneuvered majestically overhead. Their propeller whirr drifted across an empty deck.

The *Aorangi* had taken a beating. Incendiaries could not ignite fireproofed material, but had left scorches everywhere. The cabins were kindling wood. A direct hit with an explosive bomb had shattered the foremast, which lay in a tangle across the smashed sun-power collectors. The after boom trailed overside. What sails were still on the yards hung in rags. A near miss had opened two compartments in the port hull, so that the trimaran was low on that side, the deck crazily tilted.

Three dead men sprawled amidships in a black spatter of clotting blood. Ranu recollected with Alisabeta's horror: when an aircraft sank grapnels into the fore-skysail and soldiers came swarming down ropes, she hosed them with stones. Most had dropped overboard, but those three hit with nauseating sounds. Then Keanua, at the catapult, put four separate fire-shells into the gasbag. Even against modern safety devices, that served to touch off the hydrogen. The aircraft cast loose and drifted slowly seaward. The flames were pale, nearly invisible in the light, but steam puffed high when it ditched. The Maurai, naturally made no attempt to hinder the rescue operation that followed. Later the Beneghalis had been content with bombing and strafing. Once the defenders were out of action, they could board with no difficulty.

"They aren't pressing the attack as hard as they might," Keanua reported. *"But then, they hope to spare our prisoners, and don't know we have reinforcements coming. If we can hold out that long—"* He sensed how close was the rapport between Ranu and the girl, and withdrew with an embarrassed apology. Still, Ranu had had time to share the pain of burns and a pellet in his shoulder.

Alisabeta crouched in the starboard slugthrower turret. It was hot and dark and vibrated with the whining flywheel. The piece of sky in her sights was fiery blue, a tatter of sail was blinding white. He felt her fear. Too many bomb splinters, too many concussion blows, had already weakened this plywood shelter. An incendiary landing just outside would not set it afire, but could pull out the oxygen. *"So, so,"* Ranu caressed her. *"I am here now."* Their hands swung the gun about.

The lead airship peeled off the formation and lumbered into view. For the most part the squadron had passed well above missile range and dropped bombs—using crude sights, luckily. But the last several passes had been strafing runs. Keanua thought that was because their explosives were nearly used up. The expenditure of high-energy chemicals had been great, even for an industrialized power like Beneghal. Alisabeta believed they were concerned for the prisoners.

No matter. Here they came!

The airship droned low above the gaunt A of the mainmast. Its shadow swooped before it. So did a pellet storm, rocks thunking, booming, skittering, the deck atremble under their impact. Alisabeta and Ranu got the enemy's forward gun turret, a thick wooden bulge on the gondola, in their sights. They pressed the pedal that engaged the feeder. Their weapon came to life with a howl. Stones flew against the wickerwork above.

From the catapult emplacement, Keanua roared. Alisabeta heard him this far aft. A brief and frightful clatter drowned him out. The airship fell off course, wobbled, veered, and drifted aside. The girl saw the port nacelle blackened and dented. Keanua had scored a direct hit on that engine, disabled it, crippled the flyer.

"Hurrao!" Ranu whooped.

Alisabeta leaned her forehead on the gun console. She shivered with exhaustion. *"How long can we go on like this? Our magazines will soon be empty. Our sun cells are almost drained, and no way to recharge them. Don't let me faint, Ranu. Hold me, my dear—"*

"It can't be much longer. Modern military airships can do a hundred kilometers per hour. The base on Car Nicbar isn't more than four hundred kilometers away. Any moment."

This moment!

Again Keanua shouted. Alisabeta dared step out on deck for a clear view, gasped, and leaned against the turret. The Beneghalis, at their altitude, had seen the menace well before now. That last assault on the *Aorangi* was made in desperation. They marshaled themselves for battle.

Still distant, but rapidly swelling, came fifteen lean golden-painted ships. Each had four spendthrift engines to drive it through the sky; each was loaded with bombs and slugs and aerial harpoons. The Beneghalis had spent their ammunition on the *Aorangi*.

As the newcomers approached, Ranu-Alisabeta made out their insignia. Not Maurai, of course; not anything, though the dragons looked rather Sinese. Rumor had long flown about a warlord in Yunnan who had accumulated sufficient force to attempt large-scale banditry. On the other hand, there were always upstart buccaneers from Buruma, Iryan, or from as far as Smalilann—

"Get back under cover," Ranu warned Alisabeta.

"Anything can happen yet." When she was safe, he sighed. *"Now my own job starts."*

"Ranu, no, you're hurt."

"They'll need a guide. Farewell for now. Tanaroa be with you . . . till I come back."

Gently, he disengaged himself. His thought flashed upward. *"Ranu Makintairu calling. Can you hear me?"*

"Loud and clear." Aruwera Samitu, chief Intelligence officer aboard the flagship, meshed minds and whistled. *"You've had a thin time of it, haven't you?"*

"Well, we've gotten off easier than we had any right to, considering how far the situation has progressed. Listen. Your data fitted into a picture which was perfectly correct, but three or four years obsolete. The Brahmards are not just building an atomic power station here. They've built it. It's operating."

"What!"

"I swear it must be." Swiftly, Ranu sketched what he had seen. *"It can't have been completed very long, or we'd be facing some real opposition. In fact, the research team is probably still busy getting a few final bugs out. But essentially the work is complete. As your service deduced, the Beneghalis didn't have the scientific resources to do this themselves, on the basis of ancient data. I'd guess they got pretty far, but couldn't quite make the apparatus go. So they imported Lorn sunna Browen. And he, with his knowledge of nuclear processes in the stars, developed a fresh approach. I can't imagine what. But . . . they've done something on this island that the whole ancient world never achieved. Controlled*

hydrogen fusion."

"*Is the plant very big?*"

"*Tremendous. But the heart seems to be in one room. A circular chamber lined with tall iron cores. I hardly dare guess how many tons of iron. They must have combed the world.*"

"*They did. That was our first clue. Our own physicists think the reaction must be contained by magnetic fields—But no time for that. The air battle's beginning. I expect we can clear away these chaps within an hour. Can you, then, guide us in?*"

"*Yes. After I've located myself. Good luck.*"

Ranu focused attention back on his immediate surroundings. Let's see, early afternoon, so that direction was west, and he'd escaped along an approximate southeasterly track. Setting his jaws against the pain in his leg, he crawled from the hollow and limped into the canebrakes.

His progress was slow, with many pauses to climb a tree and get the lay of the land. It seemed to him that he was making enough noise to rouse Nan down in watery hell. More than an hour passed before he came on a man-made path, winding between solid walls of brush. Ruts bespoke wagons, which meant it ran from some native village to the caves. By now Ranu's chest was laboring too hard for him to exercise any forester's caution. He set off along the road.

The jungle remained hot and utterly quiet. He felt he could hear anyone else approaching in plenty of time to hide. But the Annamanese caught him unexpectedly.

They leaped from an overhead branch, two dark dwarfs in loincloths, armed with daggers and blowguns. Ranu hardly glimpsed them as they fell. He had no time to think, only to react. His left hand chopped at a skinny neck. He heard a cracking sound. The native dropped like a stone.

The other one squealed and scuttered aside. Ranu drew his knife. The blowgun rose. Ranu charged. He was dimly aware of the dart as it went past his ear. It wasn't poisoned—the Annamanese left that sort of thing to the civilized nations—but it could have reached his heart. He caught the tube and yanked it away. Fear-widened eyes bulged at him. The savage pulled out his dagger and stabbed. He was not very skillful. Ranu parried the blow, taking only a minor slash on his forearm, and drove his own blade home. The native wailed. Ranu hit again.

Then there was nothing but sunlit thick silence and two bodies that looked still smaller than when they had lived. *Merciful Lesu, did I have to do this?*

Come on, Ranu. Pick up those feet of yours. He closed the staring eyes and continued on his way. When he was near the caverns, he found a hiding place and waited.

Not for long. Such Beneghali aircraft as did not go into the sea fled. They took a stand above Port Arberta, prepared to defend it against slavers. But the Maurai left a guard at hover near the watership and cruised on past, inland over the hills. Ranu resumed contact with Aruwera, who relayed instructions to the flagship navigation officer. Presently the raiders circled above the power laboratory.

Soldiers—barbarically painted and clad—went down by parachute. The fight on the ground was bitter but short. When the last sentry had run into the woods, the Maurai swarmed through the installation.

In the cold fluorescent light that an infinitesimal fraction of its output powered, Aruwera looked upon the fusion reactor with awe. "What a thing!" he kept breathing. "What a *thing!*"

"I hate to destroy it," said his chief scientific aide. "Tanaroa! I'll have bad dreams for the rest of my life. Can't we at least salvage the plans?"

"If we can find them in time to microphotograph," Aruwera said. "Otherwise they'll have to be burned as part of the general vandalism. Pirates wouldn't steal blueprints. We've got to wreck everything as if for the sake of the iron and whatever else looks commercially valuable . . . load the loot and be off before the whole Beneghali air force arrives from the mainland. And, yes, send a signal to dismantle the Car Nicbar base. Let's get busy. Where's the main shutoff switch?"

The scientist began tracing circuits fast and knowingly, but with revulsion still in him. "How much did this cost?" he wondered. "How much of this country's wealth are we robbing?"

"Quite a bit," said Ranu. He spat. "I don't care about that, though. Maybe now they can tax their peasants less. What I do care about—" He broke off. Numerous Beneghalis and some Maurai had died today. The military professionals around him would not understand how the memory hurt, of two little black men lying dead in the jungle, hardly bigger than children.

The eighth International Physical Society convention was held in Wellantoa. It was more colorful than previous ones, for several other nations (tribes, clans, alliances, societies, religions, anarchisms . . . whatever the more or less political unit might be in a particular civilization) had now developed to the point of supporting physicists. Robes, drawers, breastplates, togas joined the accustomed sarongs and tunics and kilts. At night, music on a dozen different scales wavered from upper-level windows. Those who belonged to poetically minded cultures struggled to translate each other's compositions, and often took the basic idea into their own repertory. On the professional side, there were a number of outstanding presentations, notably a Maurai computer that used artificial organic tissue and a Brasilean mathematician's generalized theory of turbulence processes.

Lorn sunna Browen was a conspicuous attender. Not that many people asked him about his Thrilling Adventure with the Pirates. That had been years ago, after all, and he'd given short answers from the first. "They kept us on some desert island till the ransom came, then they set us off near Port Arberta after dark. We weren't mistreated. Mainly we were bored." Lorn's work on stellar evolution was more interesting.

However, the big balding man disappeared several times from the convention lodge. He spoke to odd characters down on the waterfront; money went from hand to hand; at last he got a message that brought a curiously grim chuckle from him. Promptly he went into the street and hailed a pedicab.

He got out at a house in the hills above the city. A

superb view of groves and gardens sloped down to the harbor, thronged with masts under the afternoon sun. Even in their largest town, the Sea People didn't like to be crowded. This dwelling was typical: white-washed brick, red tile roof, riotous flowerbeds. A pennant on the flagpole, under the Cross and Stars, showed that a shipmaster lived here.

When he was home. But the hired prowler had said Captain Makintairu was currently at sea. His wife had stayed ashore this trip, having two children in school and a third soon to be born. The Merican dismissed the cab and strode over the path to the door. He knocked.

The door opened. The woman hadn't changed much, he thought: fuller of body, a patch of gray in her hair, but otherwise— He bowed. "Good day, my lady Alisabeta," he said.

"Oh!" Her mouth fell open. She swayed on her feet. He was afraid she was about to faint. The irony left him.

"I'm sorry," he exclaimed. He caught her hands. She leaned on him an instant. "I'm so sorry. I never meant—I mean—"

She took a long breath and straightened. Her laugh was shaky. "You surprised me for fair," she said. "Come in."

He followed her. The room beyond was sunny, quiet, book-lined. She offered him a chair. "W-w-would you like a glass of beer?" She bustled nervously about. "Or I can make some tea. If you'd rather. That is . . . tea. Coffee?"

"Beer is fine, thanks." His Maurai was fairly fluent; any scientist had to know that language. "How've you been?"

"V-very well. And you?"

"All right."

A stillness grew. He stared at his knees, wishing he hadn't come. She put down two glasses of beer on a table beside him, took a chair opposite, and regarded him for a long while. When finally he looked up, he saw she had drawn on some reserve of steadiness deeper than his own. The color had returned to her face. She even smiled.

"I never expected you would find us, you know," she said.

"I wasn't sure I would myself," he mumbled. "Thought I'd try, though, as long as I was here. No harm in trying, I thought. Why didn't you change your name or your home base or something?"

"We considered it. But our mission had been so ultrasecret. And Makintairu is a common N'Zealanner name. We didn't plan to do anything but sink back into the obscurity of plain sailor folk. That's all we ever were, you realize."

"I wasn't sure about that. I thought from the way you handled yourselves—I figured you for special operatives."

"Oh, heavens, no. Intelligence had decided the truth was less likely to come out if the advance agents were a bona fide merchant crew, that had never been involved in such work before and never would be again. We got some training for the job, but not much, really."

"I guess the standard of the Sea People is just plain high, then," Lorn said. "Must come from generations of taking genetics into consideration when couples want to have kids, eh? That'd never work in my culture, I'm sorry to say. Not the voluntary way you do it, anyhow. We're too damned possessive."

"But we could never do half the things you've accomplished," she replied. "Desert reclamation, for instance. We simply couldn't organize that many people that efficiently for so long a time."

He drank half his beer and fumbled in a breast pocket for a cigar. "Can you satisfy my curiosity on one point?" he asked. "These past years I've wondered and wondered about what happened. I can only figure your bunch must have been in direct contact with each other. Your operation was too well coordinated for anything else. And yet you weren't packing portable radios. Are you telepaths, or what?"

"Goodness, no!" She laughed, more relaxed every minute. "We did have portable radios. Ultraminiaturized sets, surgically implanted, using body heat for power. Hooked directly into the nervous system, and hence using too broad a band for conventional equipment to read. It was rather like telepathy, I'll admit. I missed the sensation when the sets were removed afterward."

"Hm." Somewhat surer of his own self, he lit the cigar and squinted at her through the first smoke. "You're spilling your secrets mighty freely on such short notice, aren't you?"

"The transceivers aren't a secret any longer. That's more my professional interest than yours, and you've been wrapped up in preparations for your convention, so evidently you haven't heard. But the basic techniques were released last year, as if freshly invented. The psychologists are quite excited about it as a research and therapeutic tool."

"I see. And as for the fact my lab was not raided by corsairs but by an official Federation party—" Lorn's mouth tightened under the moustache. "You're confessing that too, huh?"

"What else can I do, now you've found us? Kill you? There was far too much killing." Her hand stole across the table until it rested on his. The dark eyes softened; he saw a trace of tears. "Lorn," she murmured, "we hated our work."

"I suppose." He sat quiet, looked at his cigar end, drew heavily on the smoke, and looked back at her. "I was nearly as bitter as Dhananda at first . . . bitter as the whole Brahmard caste. The biggest accomplishment of my life, gone. Not even enough notes left to reconstruct the plans. No copies had been sent to the mainland, you see, for security reasons. We were afraid of spies; or someone might have betrayed us out of sheer hysteria, associating nuclear energy with the Judgment. Though, supposing we had saved the blueprints, there'd have been no possibility of rebuilding. Beneghal's treasury was exhausted. People were starving, close to revolt in some districts, this had been so expensive, and nothing ever announced to show for their taxes. Did you stop to think of that? That you were robbing Beneghali peasants who never did you any harm?"

"Often," she said. "But remember, the tax collectors had skinned them first. The cost of that reactor project would have bought them a great deal of happiness and advancement. As witness the past several years, after the Brahmards buckled down to attaining more modest goals."

"But the reactor was working! Unlimited energy.

In ten years' time, Beneghal could've been overflowing with every industrial material. The project would have paid off a thousand times over. And you smashed it!''

Lorn sank back in his chair. Slowly, his fist unclenched. ''We couldn't prove the job had not been done by pirates,'' he said without tone. ''Certainly Beneghal couldn't declare war on the mighty Maurai Federation without proof enough to bring in a lot of indignant allies. Especially when your government offered such a whopping big help to relieve the famine . . . But we could suspect. We could feel morally certain. And angry. God, how angry!

''Until—'' He sighed. ''I don't know. When I came home and got back into the swing of my regular work . . . and bit by bit re-realized what a decent, helpful, ungreedy bunch your people always have been . . . I finally decided you must've had some reason that seemed good to you. I couldn't imagine what, but . . . oh, I don't know. Reckon we have to take some things on faith, or life would get too empty. Don't worry, Alisabeta. I'm not going to make any big public revelation. Wouldn't do any good, anyway. Too much water's gone under that particular dam. Your government might be embarrassed, but no one would care enough to make real trouble. Probably most folks would think I was lying. So I'll keep my mouth shut.'' He raised blue eyes that looked like a child's, a child who has been struck without knowing what the offense was. ''But could you tell me why? What you were scared of?''

''Surely,'' said Alisabeta. She leaned farther across the table, smiled with great gentleness, and stroked his cheek, just once. "Poor well-meaning man!

"There's no secret about our motives. The only secret is that we did take action. Our arguments have been known for decades—ever since the theoretical possibility of controlled hydrogen fusion began to be seriously discussed. That's why the Brahmards were so furtive about their project. They knew we'd put pressure on to stop them."

"Yes, Dhananda always said you were jealous. Afraid you'd lose your position as the world's top power."

"Well, frankly, that's part of it. By and large, we like the way things are going. We want to stay able to protect what we like. We weren't afraid Beneghal would embark on a career of world conquest or any such stupidity. But given atomic energy, they could manufacture such quantities of war matériel as to be invincible—explosives, motor vehicles, jet planes, yes, nuclear weapons. Once they presented us with a _fait accompli_ like that, we wouldn't be able to do anything about events. Beneghal would take the lead. Our protests could be ignored; eventually, no one anywhere would listen to us. We could only regain leadership by embarking on a similar program. And the War of Judgment proved where a race like that would end!"

"M-m-m . . . yes—"

"Even if we refrained from trying for a nuclear capability, others would not. You understand that's why the Brahmards never have told the world what they were doing. They see as well as us the scramble to duplicate their feat that would immediately follow.

"But there's a subtle and important reason why Beneghal in particular shouldn't be allowed to dominate the scene. The Brahmards are missionaries at heart. They think the entire planet should be converted to their urban-industrial ideal. Whereas we believe—and we have a good deal of psychodynamic science to back us—we believe the many different cultures that grew up in isolation during the dark ages should continue their own evolution. Think, Lorn. The most brilliant eras of history were always when alien societies came into reasonably friendly contact. When Egypt and Crete met in the Eighteenth Dynasty; Phoenician, Persian, Greek in classical times; Nippon and Sina in the Nara period; Byzantium, Asia, and Europe crossbreeding to make the Renaissance—and, yes, our era right now!

"Oh, surely, the Brahmard approach has much to offer. We don't want to suppress it. Neither do we want it to take over the world. But given the power and productivity, the speed and volume of traffic, the resource consumption, the population explosion . . . given everything that your project would have brought about . . . the machine culture *would* absorb the whole human race again. As it did before the Judgment. Not by conquest, but by being so much stronger materially that everyone would have to imitate it or go under."

Breathless, Alisabeta reached for her glass. Lorn rubbed his chin. "M-m-m . . . maybe," he said. "If industrialism can feed and clothe people better, though, doesn't it deserve to win out?"

"Who says it can?" she argued. "It can feed and clothe more people, yes. But not necessarily better.

And are sheer numbers any measure of quality, Lorn? Don't you want to leave some places on Earth where a man can go to be alone?

"And, too, suppose industrialism did begin to spread. Think of the transition period. I told you once about the horrors that are a matter of historical record, when the ancient Communists set out to westernize their countries overnight. That would happen again. Not that the Brahmards would do it; they're good men. But other leaders elsewhere—half barbarian, childishly eager for power and prestige, breaking their home cultures to bits in their impatience—such leaders would arise.

"Of course it's wrong that people go poor and hungry. But that problem has more than one solution. Each civilization can work out its own. We do it in the Islands by exploiting the seas and limiting our population. You do it in Merica by dry farming and continental trade. The Okkaidans do it by making moderation into a way of life. The Sberyaks are developing a fascinating system of reindeer ranches. And on and on. How much we learn from each other!"

"Even from Beneghal," Lorn said dryly.

"Yes," she nodded, quite grave. "Machine techniques especially. Although . . . well, let them do as they please, but no one in the Islands envies them. I really don't think their way—the old way—is anything like the best. Man isn't made for it. If industrialism was so satisfying, why did the industrial world commit suicide?"

"I suppose that's another reason you're afraid of atomic energy," he said. "Atomic war."

She shook her head. "We aren't afraid. We could develop the technology ourselves and keep anyone else from doing so. But we don't want that tight a control on the world. We think Maurai interference should be kept to an absolute minimum."

"Nevertheless," he said, sharp-toned, "you do interfere."

"True," she agreed. "That's another lesson we've gotten from history. The ancients could have saved themselves if they'd had the courage—been hard-hearted enough—to act before things snowballed. If the democracies had suppressed every aggressive dictatorship in its infancy; or if they had simply enforced their ideal of an armed world government at the time when they had the strength to do— Well." She glanced down. Her hand left his and went slowly across her abdomen; a redness crept into her cheeks. "No," she said, "I'm sorry people got hurt, that day at Annaman, but I'm not sorry about the end result. I always planned to have children, you see."

Lorn stirred. His cigar had gone out. He relit it. The first puff was as acrid as expected. Sunlight slanted in the windows to glow on the wooden floor, on a batik rug from Smatra and a statuette of strangely disturbing beauty from somewhere in Africa.

"Well," he said, "I told you I've dropped my grudge. I guess you don't figure to hold atomic energy down forever."

"Oh no. Someday, in spite of everything we do, Earth will have grown unified and dull. Then it will again be time to try for the stars."

"So I've heard various of your thinkers claim. Me,

though . . . philosophically, I don't like your attitude. I'm resigned to it, sure. Can't have every wish granted in this life. I did get the fun of working on that project, at least. But damn it, Alisabeta, I think you're wrong. If your society can't handle something big and new like the tamed atom, why, by Oktai, you've proved your society isn't worth preserving."

He felt instantly regretful and started to apologize: no offense meant, just a difference of viewpoint and — But she didn't give him a chance to say the words. She raised her head, met his gaze, and smiled like a cat.

"Our society can't handle something new?" she murmured. "Oh, my dear Lorn, what do you think we were doing that day?"

WINDMILL

—and though it was night, when land would surely be colder than sea, we had not looked for such a wind as sought to thrust us away from Calforni. Our craft shuddered and lurched. Wickerwork creaked in the gondola, rigging thrummed, the gasbag boomed, propeller noise mounted to a buzz saw whine. From my seat I glimpsed, by panel lights whose dimness was soon lost in shadows, now taut were the faces of Taupo and Wairoa where they battled to keep control, how sweat ran down their necks and bare chests and must be drenching their sarongs even in this chill.

Yet we moved on. Through the port beside me I saw ocean glimmer yield to gray and black, beneath high stars. A deeper dark, blotted far inland, must be the ruins of Losanglis. The few fires which twinkled there gave no comfort, for the squatters are known to be robbers and said to be cannibals. No Merican lord has ever tried to pacify that concrete wilderness; all who have claimed the territory have been content to cordon its dwellers off in their misery. I wonder if we Sea People should—

But I drift, do I not, Elena Kalakaua? Perhaps I write that which you have long been aware of. Forgive me. The world is so big and mysterious, civilization so thin a web across it, bound together by a few radio links and otherwise travel which is so slow, it's hard to be sure what any one person knows of it, even a best-beloved girl whose father is in Parliament. Let me drift, then. You have never been outside the happy islands of the Maurai Federation. I want to give you something of the feel, the reality, of this my last mission.

I was glad when meganecropolis fell aft out of sight and we neared the clean Muahvay. But then Captain Bowenu came to me. His hair glowed white in the gloom, yet he balanced himself with an ease learned during a youth spent in the topmasts of ships. "I'm afraid we must let you off sooner than planned," he told me. "This head wind's making the motors gulp power, and the closest recharging station is in S'Anton."

Actually it was northward, at Sannacruce. But we couldn't risk letting the Overboss there know of our presence—when that which I sought lay in country he said was his. The Meycan realm was safely distant and its Dons friendly.

One dare not let the accumulators of an aircraft get too low. For a mutinous moment I wished we could have come in a jet. But no, I understand well, such machines are too few, too precious, above all too prodigal of metal and energy; they must be reserved for the Air Force. I only tell you this passing mood of mine because it may help give you sympathy for my victims. Yes, my victims.

"Indeed, Rewi Bowenu," I said. "May I see the map?"

"Of course, Toma Nakamuha." Sitting down beside me, he spread a chart across our laps and pinpointed our location. "If you bear east-northeast, you should reach Hope before noon. Of course, your navigation can't be too accurate, with neither compass nor timepiece. But the terrain shouldn't throw you so far off course that you can't spy the windmills when they come over your horizon."

He left unspoken what would follow if he was wrong or I blundered. Buzzards, not gulls, would clean my bones, and they would whiten very far from our sea.

But the thought of those windmills and what they could mean nerved me with anger. Also, you know how Wiliamu Hamilitonu was my comrade from boyhood. Together we climbed after coconuts, prowled gillmasked among soft-colored corals and fanciful fish, scrambled up Mauna Loa to peer down its throat, shipped on a trimaran trader whose sails bore us around this whole glorious globe till we came back to Awaii and drank rum and made love to you and Lili beneath an Island moon. Wiliamu had gone before me, seeking to learn on behalf of us all what laired in the settlement that called itself Hope. He had not returned, and now I did not think he ever would.

That is why I volunteered, yes, pulled ropes for the

task. The Service had other men available, some better qualified, maybe. But we are always so short of hands that I did not need to wrangle long. When will they see in Wellantoa how undermanned we are, in this work which matters more than any other?

I unbuckled, collected my gear, and went to hang on a strap by an exit hatch. The craft slanted sharply downward. Cross-currents tore at us like an orca pack at a right whale. I hardly noticed, being busy in a last-minute review of myself.

Imagine me: tall for the Meycan I would claim to be, but not impossibly so, and you yourself have remarked on the accidents of genetics which have blent parts of my ancestry in a jutting Inio-like nose and coppery skin. Language and manners: In sailor days I was often in Meycan ports, and since joining the Service have had occasion to visit the hinterlands in company with natives. Besides, the deserts are a barrier between them and Calforni which is seldom crossed. My Spanyol and behavior ought to pass. Dress: shirt, trousers, uniform jacket, serape, sombrero, boots, all worn and dirty. Equipment: bedroll, canteen, thin pack of dried-out rations, knife, *spada* slung across back for possible machete work or self-defense. I hoped greatly I would not need it for that last. We learn the use of weapons, as well as advanced judo and karate arts, in training; nonetheless, the thought of opening up human flesh made a knot in my guts.

But what had been done to Wiliamu?

Maybe nothing. Maybe Hope was altogether innocent. We could not call in the armed forces unless we were certain. Even under the Law of Life, even under our covenant with the Overboss of Sannacruce, not even the mighty Maurai Federation can invade foreign territory like that without provoking a crisis. Not to speak of the hurt and slain, the resources and energy. We *must* be sure it was worth the cost— Now I do go astray, telling this to a politician's daughter who's spent as much time in N'Zealann as Awaii. I am too deeply back in my thoughts, as I clung there waiting.

"Level off!" Taupo sang from his seat forward. The ship struggled to a somewhat even keel. Evidently the altimeter said we were in rope's length of the ground.

Rewi, who had been beside me, squeezed my shoulder. "Tanaroa be with you, Toma," he murmured underneath the racket. He traced a cross. "Lesu Haristi deliver you from evil."

Wairoa laughed and called: "No need for deliverance from shark-toothed Nan! You'd never catch him in those dunes!" He must always have his joke. Yet his look at me was like a handclasp.

We opened the hatch and cast out a weighted line. When its windlass had stopped spinning, I threw a final glance around the cabin. I wouldn't see this gaiety of tapa and batik soon again, if ever. Supposing Hope proved harmless, I'd still have to make my own way, with mule train after mule train from trading post to trading post, to Sandago and our agents there. It would not do to reveal myself as a Maurai spy and ask to use Hope's transmitter to call for an airlift. That would make other people, elsewhere around the world, too suspicious of later strangers in their midst. (You realize, Elena, this letter is for none save you.)

"Farewell, shipmate," the men said together; and as I went out and down the rope, I heard them begin the Luck-Wishing Song.

The wind tore it from me. That was a tricky passage down, when the cord threshed like an eel and I didn't want to burn the hide off my palms. But at last I felt earth underfoot. I shook a signal wave up the rope, stepped back and watched.

For a minute the long shape hung over me, a storm cloud full of propeller thunder. Then the line was gathered in and the craft rose. It vanished astonishingly fast.

I looked around. Deserts had never much appealed to me. But this one was different: natural, not man-made. Life had not died because water was gone, top-soil exhausted, poisons soaked into the ground. Here it had had all the geological time it needed to grow into a spare environment.

The night was as clear as I've ever seen, fantastic with stars, more stars than there was crystal blackness in between them, and the Milky Way a torrent. The land reached pale under heaven-glow, speckled by silver-gray of scattered sagebrush and black weird outlines of joshua trees; I could see across its rises and arroyos to hills on the horizon, which stood blue. The wind was cold, flowing under my thin fluttering garments and around my flesh, but down here it did not shout, it murmured, and pungencies were borne upon it. From afar I heard coyotes yip. When I moved, the sandy soil crunched and gave a little beneath my feet, as alive in its own way as water.

I picked my guiding constellations out of the swarm overhead and started to walk.

Dawn was infinitely shadowed, in that vast wrinkled land. I saw a herd of wild sheep and rejoiced in the grandeur of their horns. The buzzard which took station high up in sapphire was no more terrible than my gulls, and no less beautiful. An intense green darkness against rockslopes red and tawny meant stands of piñon or juniper.

And it was April. My travels around western Meyco had taught me to know some of the wildflowers I came upon wherever shade and moisture were: bold ocotillo, honey-hued nolina plume, orchids clustered around a tiny spring. Most, shy beneath the sage and greasewood and creosote bush, I did not recognize by name. I've heard them called bellyflowers, because you have to get down on your belly to really see and love them. It amazed me how many they were, and how many kinds.

Lesser animals scuttered from me, lizards, snakes, mantises; dragonflies hovered over that mini-oasis on wings more splendid than an eagle's; I surprised a jackrabbit, which went lolloping off with a special sort of gracefulness. But a couple of antelope surprised me in turn, because I was watching a dogfight between a hawk and a raven while I strode. Suddenly I rounded a clump of chaparral and we found each other. The first antelope I'd ever met, they were delightful as dolphins and almost as fearless: because I was not wolf or grizzly or cougar; their kind had forgotten mine, which had not come slaughtering since the War of Judgment. At least, not until lately—

I discovered that I cared for the desert, not as a thing which the books said was integral to the whole regional ecology, but as a miracle.

(Oh, it isn't our territory, Elena. We'll never want to live there.) Risen, the sun hammered on my temples and speared my eyeballs, the air seethed me till my mouth was gummed, sand crept into my boots to chew my feet and the jumping cholla lived up to its name, fang-sharp burrs coming at me from no-where. Give me Mother Ocean and her islands. But I think one day I'll return for a long visit. And . . . if Wiliamu had lost his way or perished in a sand-storm or otherwise come to natural grief in these reaches, as the Hope folk said he must have done . . . was that a worse death than on the reefs or down into the deeps?

—Rewi Bowenu had been optimistic. The time was midafternoon and the land became a furnace before I glimpsed the windmills. Their tall iron skeletons wavered through heat-shimmer. Nonetheless I felt a chill. Seven of them were much too many.

Hope was a thousand or so adults and their chil-dren. It was white-washed, red-tiled adobes centered on a flagged plaza where a fountain played: no ex-travagance in this dominion of dryness, for vision has its own thirst, which that bright leaping slaked. (Flower beds as well as vegetable gardens surrounded most houses, too.) It was irrigation ditches fanning outward to turn several square kilometers vivid with crops and orchards.

And it was the windmills.

They stood on a long hill behind the town, to catch every shift of air. Huge they were. I could but guess at the man-years of toil which had gone into shaping them, probably from ancient railway tracks or bridge girders hauled across burning emptiness, reforged by the muscles of men who themselves could not be bent. Ugly they were, and in full swing they filled my ears with harsh creakings and groanings. But beauty and quietness would come, I was told. This community had been founded a decade and a half ago. The first several years had gone for barebones survival. Only of late could people begin to take a little ease, think beyond time's immediate horizon.

Behind the hill, invisible from the town, stood a large shedlike building. From it, handmade ceramic pipes, obviously joined to the mill system, led over the ridge to a great brick tank, just below the top on this side. From that tank in turn, sluices fed the canals, the dwellings and workshops, and—via a penstock—a small structure at the foot of the hill which Danil Smit said contained a hydroelectric generator. (Some days afterward, I was shown that machine. It was pre-Judgment. The labor of dragging it here from its ancient site and reconstructing it must have broken hearts.)

He simply explained at our first encounter: "The mills raise water from the spring, you see, it bein' too low for proper irrigation. On the way down again, the flow powers that dynamo, which charges portable accumulators people bring there. This way we get a steady supply of electricity, not big, but enough for lights an' such." (Those modern Everlast fluorescents were almost shockingly conspicuous in homes where almost everything else was as primitive as any woodsrunner's property.)

"Why do you not use solar screens?" I asked. "Your power supply would be limited only by the number of square meters you could cover with them."

My pronunciation of their dialect of Ingliss passed quite easily for a Spanyol accent. As for vocabulary, well, from the start I hadn't pretended to be an ordinary wandering worker. I was Miwel Artuba y Gonsals, of a *rico* family in Tamico, fallen on ill days when our estates were plundered during the Watemalan War. Trying to mend my fortunes, I enlisted with a mercenary company. We soldiered back and forth across the troubled lands, Tekkas, Zona, Vada, Ba-Calforni, till the disaster at Montrey, of which the *señores* had doubtless heard, from which I counted myself lucky to escape alive . . . .

Teeth gleamed in Smit's beard. "Ha! Usin' what for money to buy 'em? Remember, we had to start here with no more'n we could bring in oxcarts. Everything you see around you was dug, forged, sawed an' dovetailed together, fire-baked, planted, plowed, cultivated, harvested, threshed, with these."

He held out his hands, and they were like the piñon boles, strong, hard, but unmercifully gnarled. I watched his eyes more, though. In that shaggy, craggy face they smoldered with a prophet's vision.

Yet the mayor of Hope was no backwoods fanatic. Indeed, he professed indifference to rite and creed. "Oktai an' his fellow gods are a bunch of Asians, an' Calforni threw out the Mong long ago," he remarked once to me. "As for Tanaroa, Lesu Haristi, an' that lot, well, the sophisticated thing nowadays in Sannacruce is to go to their church, seein' as how the Sea

People do. No disrespect to anybody's faith, understand. I know you Meycans also worship—uh—Esu Carito, is that what you call him? But me, my trust is in physics, chemistry, genetics, an' a well-trained militia.'' For he had been a prosperous engineer in the capital, before he led the migration hither.

I would have liked to discuss philosophy with him and, still more, applied science. It's so hard to learn how much knowledge of what kind has survived, even in the upper classes of a realm with which we have as regular intercourse as we do with Sannacruce.

Do you fully realize that? Many don't. I didn't, till the Service academy and Service experience had educated me. You can't help my sorrow unless you know its source. Let me therefore spell out what we both were taught as children, in order then to point out how over-simplified it is.

The War of Judgment wiped out a number of cities, true; but most simply died on the vine, in the famines, plagues and worldwide political collapse which followed; and the reason for the chaos was less direct destruction than it was the inability of a resources-impoverished planet to support a gross overpopulation when the industrial machinery faltered for just a few years. (The more I see and ponder, the more I believe those thinkers are right who say that crowding, sensory deprivation, loss of all touch with a living world in which mankind evolved as one animal among millions—that that very unnaturalness brought on the mass lunacy which led to thermonuclear war. If this be true, my work is sacred. Help me never to believe, Elena, that any of the holiness has entered my own self.)

Well, most of the books, records, even technical apparatus remained, being too abundant for utter destruction. Thus, during the dark centuries, barbarians might burn whole libraries to keep alive through a winter; but elsewhere, men preserved copies of the same works, and the knowledge of how to read them. When a measure of stability returned, in a few of the least hard-hit regions, it was not ignorance which kept people from rebuilding the old high-energy culture.

It was lack of resources. The ancestors used up the rich deposits of fuel and minerals. Then they had the means to go on to exploit leaner substances. But once their industrial plant had stopped long enough to fall into decay, it was impossible to reconstruct. This was the more true because nearly all human effort must go into merely keeping half-alive, in a world whose soil, water, forests and wildlife had been squandered.

If anything, we are more scientific nowadays, we are more ingenious engineers, than ever men were before—we islands of civilization in the barbarian swamp which slowly, slowly we try to reclaim—but we must make do with what we have, which is mostly what the sun and living things can give us. The amount of that is measured by the degree to which we have nursed Earth's entire biosphere back toward health.

Thus the text we offer children. And it is true, of course. It's just not the whole truth.

You see—this is the point I strive to make, Elena, this is why I started by repeating the tricky obvious —our machinations are only one small force in a typhoon of forces. Traveling, formerly as a sailor, now as an agent of the Ecological Service, I have had borne in upon me how immense the world is, how various and mysterious. We look through Maurai eyes. How well do those see into the soul of the Calfornian, Meycan, Orgonian, Stralian . . . of folk they often meet . . . and what have they glimpsed of the depths of Sudamerca, Africa, Eurasia? We may be the only great power; but we are, perhaps, ten million among, perhaps, twenty times our number; and the rest are strangers to us, they were blown on different winds during the dark centuries, today they begin to set their own courses and these are not ours.

Maurai crewmen may carouse along the waterfront of Sannacruce. Maurai captains may be invited to dine at the homes of merchants, Maurai admirals with the Overboss himself. But what do we know of what goes on behind the inner walls, or behind the faces we confront?

Why a bare three years ago we heard a rumor that an emigrant colony was flourishing in the Muahvay fringe. Only one year ago did we get around to verifying this from the air, and seeing too many windmills, and sending Wiliamu Hamilitonu to investigate and die.

Well, I would, as I said, have liked to talk at length with this intelligent and enigmatic man, Mayor Danil Smit. But my role as a *cab'llero* forbade. Let my tale go on.

They had received me with kindness in the settlement. Eager curiosity was there too, of course. Their communal radio could pick up broadcasts from

Sannacruce city; but they had turned their backs on Sannacruce, and anyhow, it's not what we would call a thriving cultural center. Periodic trips to trading posts maintained by the Sandagoan Mercanteers, albeit the caravans brought books and journals back among the supplies, gave no real satisfaction to their news-hunger. Besides, having little to barter with and many shortages of necessities, they could not afford much printed matter.

Yes they seemed, on the whole, a happy folk.

Briun Smit, son of Danil, and his wife Jeana gave me lodging. I shared the room of their five living children, but that was all right, those were good, bright youngsters; it was only that I was hard put to invent enough adventures of Lieutenant Arruba for them, when we lay together on rustling cornshuck pallets and they whispered and giggled in the dark before sleep or the dawn before work.

Briun was taller, leaner and blonder than his father, and seemingly less fervent. He cultivated hardly any land, preferring to serve the community as a ranger. This was many things: to ride patrol across the desert against possible bandits, to guard the caravans likewise when they traveled, to prospect for minerals, to hunt bighorn, antelope and mustang for meat. Besides crossbow and blowgun, he was deadly expert with ax, recurved hornbow, sling, lasso and bolas. The sun had leathered him still more deeply than his neighbors and carved crow's-feet around his eyes. His clothes were the general dull color—scant dyestuff was being made thus far—but flamboyant in cut and drape and in the cockade he bore on his curve-brimmed hat.

"Sure, Don Miwel, you just stay with me long's you've a mind to," he said out of the crowd which gathered when I made my dusty way into town.

"I fear I lack the skill to help you at farming, sir," I answered quite truthfully. "But perhaps I have some at carpentry, ropework and the like," which every sailor must and a landed aristocrat might.

Jeana was soon as delighted by what I could do as by what I could tell. It pleased me to please her— for instance, by making a bamboo-tube sprinkler grid for her garden, or a Hilsch arrangement out of sheet metal not immediately needed elsewhere, that really cooled the house whenever the frequent winds blew, or by telling her that Maurai scientists had developed insects and germs to prey on specific plant pests and how to order these through the Mercanteers. She was a small woman, but beautifully shaped beneath the drab gown, of elfin features and vivid manner and a fair complexion not yet bleached by the badlands.

"You have a lovely wife, *señor*, if I may so," I remarked to Briun, the second evening at his home. We sat on the verandah, taking our ease after the day's jobs. Our feet were on the rail, we had pipes in our right hands and mugs of cider in our left, which she had fetched us. Before us stood only a couple of other houses, this one being on the edge of town; beyond gleamed the canals, palm trees swaying along their banks, the first shoots of grain an infinitely delicate green, until far, far out, on the edge of sight, began the umber of untouched desert. Long light-beams cast shadows from the west and turned purple the eastern hills. It was blowing, coolness borne out of lands already nighted, and I heard the iron song of the unseen windmills.

"Thanks," the ranger said to me. He grinned. "I think the same." He took a drink and a puff before adding, slowly now and soberly: "She's a reason we're here."

"Really?" I leaned forward.

"You'd learn the story regardless. Might as well tell you right off, myself." Briun scowled. "Her father was a forester o' rank in Sannacruce. But that didn't help much when the Overboss' eye lit on her, an' she fourteen. He liked—likes 'em young, the swine. When she refused presents, he started pressurin' her parents. They held out, but everybody knew it couldn't be for long. If nothin' else, some night a gang o' bully boys would break in an' carry her off. Next mornin', done bein' done, her parents might as well accept his bribes, hopin' when he was tired of her he'd find a poor man who'd take another gift to marry her. We'd seen cases."

"Terrible," I said. And it is. Among them, it's more than an angering, perhaps frightening episode of coercion; they set such store by virginity that the victim is apt to be soul-scarred for life. My question which followed was less honest, since I already knew the answer: "Why do the citizens tolerate that kind of ruler?"

"He has the men-at-arms," Briun sighed. "An', o' course, he don't directly offend a very big percentage. Most people like bein' secure from pirates or invaders, which the bastard does give 'em. Finally, he's hand in glove with the Sea People. Long's they support him, or at least don't oppose an' boycott him, he's got the metal to hire those soldiers." He shook his head. "I can't see why they do. I really can't. The Maurai claim to be decent folk."

"I have heard," I said cautiously, "he follows their advice about things like reforestation, soil care, bio-control, wildlife management, fisheries."

"But not about human bein's!"

"Perhaps not, Mister Briun. I do not know. I do know this, however. The ancestors stripped the planet nearly to its bones. Unless and until we put flesh back, no human beings anywhere will be safe from ruin. In truth, my friend, we cannot maintain what technology we have except on a biological basis. For example, when almost everything has to be made from wood, we must keep the forests in equilibrium with the lumberers. Or, since the oil is gone, or nearly gone, we depend greatly on microbial fuel cells . . . and the fuels they consume are by-products of life, so we require abundant life. If the oil did come back—if we made some huge strike again, by some miracle—we would still not dare burn much. The ancestors found what happens when you poison the environment."

He gave me a sharp look. I realized I had stepped out of character. In haste, I laughed and said: "I have had more than one Maurai agent lecture me, in old days on our estate, you see. Now tell me, what happened in Sannacruce?"

"Well—" He relaxed, I hoped. "The discontent had been growin' for quite a while anyway, you understand. Not just Overboss Charl; the whole basic policy, which won't change while the Sea People keep their influence. We're becomin' too many to live well, when not enough fallow land or fishin' ground is bein' opened for use."

I refrained from remarks about birth control, having learned that what seems only natural to a folk who spend their lives on shipboard and on islands, comes slowly indeed to those who imagine they have a continent at their free disposal. Until they learn, they will die back again and again; we can but try to keep them from ravaging too much nature in the meantime. Thus the doctrine. But, Elena, can you picture how hard it is to apply that doctrine to living individuals, to Briun and Jeana, eager hobbledehoy Rodj and little, trusting Dorthy?

"There'd been some explorin'," he continued after another sip and another pungent blue smokeplume trailed forth into the evening. "The good country's all taken where it isn't reserved. But old books told how desert had been made to bloom, in places like Zona. Maybe a possibility closer to home? Well, turned out true. Here, in the Muahvay, a natural wellspring, ample water if it was channeled. Dunno how the ancestors missed it. My father thinks it didn't exist back then; an earthquake split the strata, sometime durin' the dark centuries, an' opened a passage to a bigger water table than had been suspected before.

"Anyhow, Jeana's case was sort of a last straw. Her dad an' mine led a few pioneers off, on a pretext. They did the basic work of enclosin' the spring, diggin' the first short canal, erectin' the first windmill an' makin' an' layin' the first pipelines. They hired nomad Inios to help, but nevertheless I don't see how they did it, an' in fact several died o' strain.

"When the rest came back, families quietly sold

out, swappin' for wagons, tools, gene-tailored seed an' such. The Overboss was took by surprise. If he'd tried to forbid the migration, he'd've had a civil war on his hands. He still claims us, but we don't pay him any tax or any mind. If ever we link up to anybody else, I reckon it'll be Sandago. But we'd rather stay independent, an' I think we can. This territory will support a big population once it's developed."

"A heroic undertaking," I said low.

"Well, a lot died in the second group, too, and a lot are half crippled from overwork in those early days, but we made it." His knuckles stood forth around the handle of his mug, as if it were a weapon. "We're self-supportin' now, an' our surplus to trade grows larger every year. We're free!"

"I admire what you have done, also as a piece of engineering," I said. "Perhaps you have ideas here we could use when at last I go home again. Or perhaps I could suggest something to you?"

"Um." He sucked on his pipe and frowned, abruptly uncomfortable.

"I would like to see your whole hydraulic system," I said; and my heart knocked within me. "Tomorrow can you introduce me to the man in charge, and I go look at the water source and the windmills?"

"*No!*" He sprang from his chair. For a moment he loomed over me, and I wondered if he'd drop his pipe and snatch the knife at his belt. Shadows were thickening and I couldn't make out his face too well, but eyes and teeth stood aglisten.

After a long few seconds he eased. His laugh was shaky as he sat down. "Sorry, Don Miwel." He was not a skilled liar. "But we've had that kind o' trouble before, which is why I, uh, overreacted." He sought solace in tobacco. "I'm afraid Windmill Ridge is off limits to everybody except the staff an' the mayor; likewise the springhouse. You see, uh, we've got just the one source, big though it is, an' we're afraid o' pollution or damage or— All right, in these lands water's worth more than blood. We can't risk any spy for a possible invader seein' how our defenses are arranged. No insult meant. You understand, don't you, guest-friend?"

Sick with sorrow, I did.

Still, the Service would require absolute proof. It seemed wise to bide my time, quietly study the layout for a few weeks, observe routines, gather bits and pieces of information, while the dwellers in Hope came fully to accept Miwel Arruba.

The trouble was, I in my turn came to accept them.

When Briun's boy Rodj told me about their winter visitor, his excitement glowed. "Clear from Awaii, he was, Miwel! A geologist, studyin' this country; an' the stories he could tell!" Quickly: "Not full of action like yours. But he's been clear around the world."

Wiliamu hadn't expected he would need a very thick cover.

Not wanting to prompt Briun's suspicion, I asked further of Jeana, one day when he was out and the children napping or at school. It bespoke a certain innocence that, despite the restrictive sexual customs, none looked askance at my hostess and me for the many hours we spent alone together. I confess it was hard for me to keep restraint—not only this long celibacy, but herself, sweet, spirited and bright, as kindled by my newness as her own children.

I'd finished the sprinkler layout and hooked it to the cistern on the flat roof. "See," I said proudly, and turned the wooden spigot. Water danced over the furrows she hoed alone. "No more lugging a heavy can around."

"Oh, Miwel!" She clapped small work-bitten hands. "I don't know how to— This calls for a celebration. We'll throw a party come Saddiday. But right now—" She caught my arm. "Come inside. I'm bakin'." The rich odors had already told me that. "You get the heels off the first loaf out o' the oven."

There was tea as well, rare and costly when it must be hauled from Sina, or around the Horn from Florda. We sat on opposite sides of a plank table, in the kitchen dimness and warmth, and smiled at each other. Sweat made tiny beads on her brow; the thin dress clung. "I wish I could offer you lemonade," she said. "This is lemonade weather. My mother used to make it, back home. She died in Sandstorm Year an' never— Well." A forlorn cheerfulness: "Lemonade demands ice, which we haven't yet."

"You will?"

"Father Danil says prob'ly nex' year we—Hope'll have means to buy a couple o' fridges, an' the power plant'll be expanded enough so we can afford to run them."

"Will you build more windmills for that?" A tingle went through me. I struggled to be casual. "Seems you already have plenty for more than your fluorolights.''

Her glance was wholly frank and calm. ''We have to pump a lot o' water. It don't gush from a mountainside, remember, it bubbles from low ground.''

I hated to risk spoiling her happiness, but duty made me press in: ''A Maurai geologist visited here not long before, I have heard. Could he not have given you good advice?''

''I . . . I don't know. That's man talk. Anyway, you heard how we can't let most of ourselves in there —I've never been—let alone strangers, even nice ones like you.''

''He would have been curious, though. Where did he go on to? Maybe I can find him later.''

''I don't know. He left sudden-like, him an' his two Inio guides. One mornin' they were gone, nary a word o' good-by except, naturally, to the mayor. I reckon he got impatient.''

Half of me wanted to shout at her: *When our ''Geological Institute'' radioed inquiries about its man, your precious village elders gave us the same answer, that he'd departed, that if he failed to arrive elsewhere he must have met with some misfortune on the way. But that wouldn't happen! Would it? An experienced traveler, two good natives at his side, well supplied, no rumor of bandits in this region for years past . . . . Have you thought about that, Jeana? Have you dared think about it?*

But the rest of me held my body still. ''More tea?'' she asked.

I am not a detective. Folk less guileless would have frozen at my questions. I did avoid putting them in the presence of fierce old Danil Smit, and others who had spent adult years in the competition and intrigues of Sannacruce city. As for the rest, however . . . they invited me to dinner, we drank and yarned, we shared songs beneath that unutterably starry sky, several times we rode forth to see a spectacular canyon or simply for the joy of riding . . . . It was no trick to niggle information out of them.

For example, I wondered aloud if they might be over-hunting the range. Under the Law of Life, it could be required that a qualified game warden be established among them, directly responsible to the International Conservation Tribunal. Briun bristled a moment, then pointed out correctly that man always upsets nature's balance when he enters a land, and that what counts is to strike a new balance. Hope was willing to keep a trained wildlife manager around; but let him be a local person, albeit educated abroad, somebody who knew local conditions. (And would keep local secrets.)

In like manner, affable men assigned to duty on Windmill Ridge told me their schedules, one by one, as I inquired when they would be free for sociability. My work for the younger Smit household had excited a great deal of enthusiasm; in explaining it, I could slip in questions about their own admirable hydraulic system. Mere details about rate of flow, equipment ordered or built, equipment hoped for—mere jigsaw fragments.

Presently I had all but the final confirmation. My eyewitness account would be needed to call in the troops. What I had gained hitherto justified the hazard in entering the forbidden place.

A caravan was being organized for Barstu trading

post. I could accompany it, and thence make my way to Sandago. And that, I trusted, I feared, would be my last sight of these unbreakable people whom I had come to love.

The important thing was that no sentry was posted after dark. The likelihood of trouble was small, the need of sleep and of strength for next day's labor was large.

I slipped from among the children. Once I stepped on a pallet in the dark, the coarseness crackled beneath my bare foot, Dorthy whimpered in her blindness and I stiffened. But she quieted. The night was altogether deserted as I padded through the memorized house, out beneath stars and a bitter-bright gibbous moon. It was cold and breezy; I heard the windmills. Afar yelped coyotes. (There were no dogs. They hadn't yet any real need for them. But soon would come the cattle and sheep, not just a few kept at home but entire herds. Then farewell, proud bighorn and soaring antelope.) The streets were gritty. I kept out of the gray-white light, stayed in the shadows of gray-white houses. Beyond the village, rocks barked my toes, sagebrush snatched at my ankles, while I trotted around to the other side of the Ridge.

There stood the low, wide adobe structure which, I was told, covered the upwelling water, to minimize loss by evaporation and downfall of alkaline dust into it. From there, I was told, it was lifted by the mills into the brick basin, from which it went to its work. Beyond the springhouse the land rolled upward, dim and empty of man. But I could make out much else, sage, joshua trees, an owl ghosting by.

My knife had electromagnetic devices built into its handle. I scarcely needed it to get in, save for not wanting to leave signs of breakage. The padlock on the door was as flimsy as the walls proved to be thin. Pioneers in a stern domain had had nothing to spare for more than the most pathetic of frauds.

I entered, closed the door behind me, flashed light from that gempommel on my knife, which was actually a lens. The air was cold in here, too. I saw moisture condensed on pipes which plunged into the clay floor and up through the roof, and somehow smelled it. Otherwise, in an enormous gloom, I barely glimpsed workbenches, toolracks, primitive machinery. I could not now hear the turning sails of the windmills which drove the pumps; but the noise of pistons in crudely fashioned tallow-lubricated cylinders was like bones sliding across each other.

There was no spring. I hadn't expected any.

A beam stabbed at me. I doused my own, reversed it to make a weapon, recoiled into murk. From behind the glare which sought about, a deep remembered voice said, more weary than victorious: "Never mind, Miwel or whoever you are. I know you haven't got a gun. I do. The town's firearm. Buckshot loaded."

Crouched among bulky things and my pulsebeats, I called back: "It will do you less than good to kill me, Danil Smit"—and shifted my position fast. The knife was keen in my hand, my thumb braced easily against the guard. I was young, in top shape, trained; I could probably take him in the dark. I didn't want to. Lesu Haristi knows how I didn't want to, and knows it was not merely for fear of having to flee ill prepared into the desert.

He sighed, like the night wind beyond these walls. "You're a Maurai spy, aren't you?"

"An agent of the Ecological Service," I answered, keeping moving. "We've treaty arrangements with the Overboss. I agree he's a rat in some ways, but he co-operates in saving his land for his great-grandchildren . . . and yours."

"We weren't sure, me an' my partners," Danil Smit said. "We figured we'd take turns watchin' here till you left. You might've been honest."

"Unlike you—you murderers." But somehow I could not put anger into that word, not even for Wiliamu my shipmate and his two nameless guides.

"I s'pose you've got backup?" he called.

"Yes, of course," I said. "Losing our first man was plenty to make us suspicious. Losing the second . . . imagine." Leap, leap went my crouch-bent legs. I prayed the noise of the pumping masked my foot-thuds from him. "It's clear what your aim is, to grow in obscurity till you're so large and strong you can defy everybody—the Federation itself—from behind your barrier of desert distances. But don't you see," I panted, "my superiors have already guessed this? And they don't propose to let the menace get that big!"

You know I exaggerated. Manpower and equipment is spread so thin, close to the breaking point. It might well be decided that there are more urgent matters than one rebellious little community. Wiliamu and I might be written off. Sweat stood chill upon me. So many seas unsailed, lands unwalked, girls unloved, risings of Orion and the Cross unseen!

"You haven't realized how determined we are," I told him. "The Law of Life isn't rhetoric, Danil Smit. It's survival."

"What about our survival?" he groaned.

"Listen," I said, "if I come out into view, can we talk before Tanaroa?"

"Huh? . . . Oh." He stood a while, and in that moment I knew what it is to be of a race who were once great and are no longer. Well, in their day *they* were the everywhere-thrusting aliens; and if they devoured the resources which were the very basis of their power, what could they expect but that Earth's new masters would come from the poor and forgotten who had had less chance to do likewise? Nevertheless, that was long ago, it was dead. Reality was Danil Smit, humbled into saying, "Yes," there in the dark of the shed, he who had seen no other way than murder to preserve his people's freedom.

I switched my own flash back on and set it down by his on a bench, to let light reflect off half-seen shapes and pick his beard and hands and pleading eyes out of the rattling, gurgling murk. I said to him, fast, because I did not like saying it:

"We suspected you weren't using a natural outflow. After centuries, the overnight discovery of such a thing would have been strange. No, what you found was a water table, and you're pumping it dry, in this land of little rain, and that breaks the Law of Life."

He stood before me, in the last rags of his patriarchy, and cried: "But why? All right, all right, eventually we'll've exhausted it. But that could be two-three hundred years from now! Don't you see, we could use that time for livin'?"

"And afterward?" I challenged, since I must keep reminding myself that my cause is right, and must make him believe that my government is truly fanatical on this subject. (He would not have met enough of our easy-going islanders to realize crusades are impossible to us—that, at most, a tiny minority of devotees strive to head off disaster at the outset, before the momentum of it has become too huge.) My life might hang upon it. The shotgun dangled yet in his grasp. He had a good chance of blasting me before I could do more than wound him.

I went on: "Afterward! Think. Instead of what life we have today, to enlarge human knowledge and, yes, the human spirit . . . instead of that, first a sameness of crops and cattle, then a swarm of two-legged ants, then barrenness. We must resist this wherever it appears. Otherwise, in the end—if we can't, as a whole species, redeem ourselves—will be an Earth given back to the algae, or an Earth as bare as the moon."

"Meanwhile, though," he said desperately, "we'd build aqueducts . . . desalinization plants . . . fusion power—"

I did not speak of rumors I have heard that controlled fusion has in fact been achieved, and been suppressed. Besides its being an Admiralty secret, if true, I had no heart to explain to the crumbling old man that Earth cannot live through a second age of energy outpouring and waste. One remote day, folk may come to know in their blood that the universe was not made for them alone; then they can safely be given the power to go to the stars. But not in our lifetimes.

Not in the lifetime that Wiliamu my comrade might have had.

I closed my teeth on the words: "The fact is, Danil Smit, this community was founded on the exhaustion of ground water vital to an entire ecology. That was a flat violation of the Law and of international covenants. To maintain it, you and your co-conspirators resorted to murder. I'll presume most of the dwellers in Hope are innocent—most believe there is a natural spring here—but where are the bodies of our men? Did you at least have the decency to give them back to the earth?"

The soul went out of him. Hope's founding father crept into my arms and wept.

I stroked his hair and whispered, "It could be worse, it could be worse. I'll work for you, don't give up," while my tears and his ran together.

After all, I will remind my admirals, we have islands to reclaim, stoninesses in the middle of a living ocean.

Give the pioneers topsoil and seeds, give them rainwater cisterns and solar stills, teach them palm and breadfruit culture and the proper ranching of the sea. Man does not have to be always the deathmaker. I know my proposal is a radical break with tradition. But it would be well—it would be a most hopeful precedent—if these, who are not of our kind, could be made into some of our strongest lifebringers.

Remember, we have an entire worldful of people, unimaginably diverse, to educate thus, if we can. We must begin somewhere.

I swore I would strive to the utmost to have this accepted. I actually dared say I thought our government could be persuaded to pardon Danil Smit and his few associates in the plot. But if an example must be made, they are ready to hang, begging only that those they have loved be granted exile instead of a return to the tyrant.

Elena, speak to your father. Speak to your friends in Parliament. Get them to help us.

But do not tell them this one last thing that happened. Only think upon it at night, as I do, until I come home again.

We trod forth when dawn was whitening the east, Danil Smit and I. Stars held out in a westward darkness, above the dunes and eldritch trees. But those were remote, driven away by fields and canals carved from the tender desert. And a mordant wind made the mills on the ridge overhead creak and clang and roar as they sucked at the planet.

He raised a hand toward them. His smile was weary and terrible. "You've won this round, Nakamuha, you an' your damned nature worshipers," he said. "My children an' children's children 'ull fit into your schemes, because you're powerful. But you won't be forever. What then, Nakamuha? What then?"

I looked up to the whirling skeletons, and suddenly the cold struck deep into me.

KITH

GHETTO

The monorail set them off at Kith Town, on the edge
of the great city. Its blaze of light, red and gold and
green looped between high slim towers, pulsed in the
sky above them, but here it was dark and still, night
had come. Kenri Shaun stood for a moment with the
others, shifting awkwardly on his feet and wondering
what to say. They knew he was going to resign, but
the Kithman's rule of privacy kept the words from
their lips.

"Well," he said at last, "I'll be seeing you
around."

"Oh, sure," said Graf Kishna. "We won't be
leaving Earth again for months yet."

After a pause, he added: "We'll miss you when we
do go. I—wish you'd change your mind, Kenri."

"No," said Kenri. "I'm staying. But thanks."

"Come see us," invited Graf. "We'll have to get a bunch together for a poker game sometime soon."

"Sure. Sure I will."

Graf's hand brushed Kenri's shoulder, one of the Kith gestures which said more than speech ever could. "Goodnight," he spoke aloud.

"Goodnight."

Words murmured in the dimness. They stood there for an instant longer, half a dozen men in the loose blue doublets, baggy trousers, and soft shoes of the Kith in Town. There was a curious similarity about them, they were all of small and slender build, dark complexioned, but it was the style of movement and the expression of face which stamped them most. They had looked on strangeness all their lives, out between the stars.

Then the group dissolved and each went his own way. Kenri started toward his father's place. There was a thin chill in the air, the northern pole was spinning into autumn, and Kenri hunched his shoulders and jammed his hands into his pockets.

The streets of the Town were narrow concrete strips, nonluminous, lit by old-style radiant globes. These threw a vague whiteness on lawns and trees and the little half-underground houses set far back from the roads. There weren't many people abroad: an elderly officer, grave in mantle and hood; a young couple walking slowly, hand in hand; a group of children tumbling on the grass; small lithe forms filling the air with their laughter, filling themselves with the beauty and mystery which were Earth. They might have been born a hundred years ago, some of those children, and looked on worlds whose very suns were invisible here, but always the planet drew men home again. They might cross the Galaxy someday, but always they would return to murmurous forests and galloping seas, rain and wind and swift-footed clouds, through all space and time they would come back to their mother.

Most of the hemispheres Kenri passed were dark, tended only by machines while their families flitted somewhere beyond the sky. He passed the home of a friend, Jong Errifrans, and wondered when he would see him again. The *Golden Flyer* wasn't due in from Betelgeuse for another Earth-century, and by then the *Fleetwing*, Kenri's own ship, might well be gone — *No, wait, I'm staying here. I'll be a very old man when Jong comes back, still young and merry, still with a guitar across his shoulders and laughter on his lips. I'll be an Earthling then.*

The town held only a few thousand houses, and most of its inhabitants were away at any given time. Only the *Fleetwing*, the *Flying Cloud*, the *High Barbaree*, the *Our Lady*, and the *Princess Karen* were at Sol now: their crews would add up to about 1200, counting the children. He whispered the lovely, archaic names, savoring them on his tongue. Kith Town, like Kith society, was changeless; it had to be. When you traveled near the speed of light and time shrank so that you could be gone a decade and come back to find a century flown on Earth—And here was home, where you were among your own kind and not a tommy who had to bow and wheedle the great merchants of Sol, here you could walk like a man. It wasn't true what they said on Earth, that tommies were rootless, without planet or history or loyalty.

There was a deeper belongingness here than the feverish rise and warring and fall of Sol could ever know.

"—Good evening, Kenri Shaun."

He stopped, jerked out of his reverie, and looked at the young woman. The pale light of a street globe spilled across her long dark hair and down her slim shape. "Oh—" He caught himself and bowed. "Good evening to you, Theye Barinn. I haven't seen you in a long time. Two years, isn't it?"

"Not quite so long for me," she said. "The *High Barbaree* went clear to Vega last trip. We've been in orbit here about an Earth-month. The *Fleetwing* got in a couple of weeks ago, didn't she?"

Covering up, not daring to speak plainly. He knew she knew almost to the hour when the great spaceship had arrived from Sirius and taken her orbit about the home planet.

"Yes," he said, "but our astrogation computer was burned out and I had to stay aboard with some others and get it fixed."

"I know," she answered. "I asked your parents why you weren't in Town. Weren't you—impatient?"

"Yes," he said, and a thinness edged his tone. He didn't speak of the fever that had burned in him, to get away, get downside, and go to Dorthy where she waited for him among the roses of Earth. "Yes, of course, but the ship came first, and I was the best man for the job. My father sold my share of the cargo for me; I never liked business anyway."

Small talk, he thought, biting back the words, chatter eating away the time he could be with

Dorthy. But he couldn't quite break away, Theye was a friend. Once he had thought she might be more, but that was before he knew Dorthy.

"Things haven't changed much since we left," she said. "Not in twenty-five Earth-years. The Star Empire is still here, with its language and its genetic hierarchy—a little bigger, a little more hectic, a little closer to revolt or invasion and the end. I remember the Africans were much like this, a generation or two before they fell."

"So they were," said Kenri. "So were others. So will still others be. But I've heard the Stars are clamping down on us."

"Yes." Her voice was a whisper. "We have to buy badges now, at an outrageous price, and wear them everywhere outside the Town. It may get worse. I think it will."

He saw that her mouth trembled a little under the strong curve of her nose, and the eyes turned up to his were suddenly filmed with a brightness of tears. "Kenri—is it true what they're saying about you?"

"Is what true?" Despite himself, he snapped it out.

"That you're going to resign? Quit the Kith—become an . . . Earthling?"

"I'll talk about it later." It was a harshness in his throat. "I haven't time now."

"But Kenri—" She drew a long breath and pulled her hand back.

"Goodnight, Theye. I'll see you later. I have to hurry."

He bowed and went on, quickly, not looking back. The lights and the shadows slid their bars across him as he walked.

Dorthy was waiting, and he would see her tonight. But just then he couldn't feel happy about it, somehow.

He felt like hell.

She had stood at the vision port, looking out into a dark that crawled with otherness, and the white light of the ship's walls had been cool in her hair. He came softly behind her and thought again what a wonder she was. Even a millennium ago, such tall slender blondes had been rare on Earth. If the human breeders of the Star Empire had done nothing else, they should be remembered with love for having created her kind.

She turned around quickly, sensing him with a keeness of perception he could not match. The silver-blue eyes were enormous on him, and her lips parted a little, half covered by one slim hand. He thought what a beautiful thing a woman's hand was. "You startled me, Kenri Shaun."

"I am sorry, Freelady," he said contritely.

"It—" She smiled with a hint of shakiness. "It is nothing. I am too nervous—don't know interstellar space at all."

"It can be . . . unsettling, I suppose, if you aren't used to it, Freelady," he said. "I was born between the stars, myself."

She shivered faintly under the thin blue tunic. "It is too big," she said. "Too big and old and strange for us, Kenri Shaun. I thought traveling between the planets was something beyond human understand-

ing, but this—'' Her hand touched his, and his fingers closed on it, almost against his own will. "This is like nothing I ever imagined."

"When you travel nearly at the speed of light," he said, covering his shyness with pedantry, "you can't expect conditions to be the same. Aberration displaces the stars, and Doppler effect changes the color. That's all, Freelady."

The ship hummed around them, as if talking to herself. Dorthy had once wondered what the vessel's robot brain thought—what it felt like to be a spaceship, forever a wanderer between foreign skies. He had told her the robot lacked consciousness, but the idea had haunted him since. Maybe only because it was Dorthy's idea.

"It's the time shrinking that frightens me most, perhaps," she said. Her hand remained in his, the fingers tightening. He sensed the faint wild perfume she wore, it was a heady draught in his nostrils. "You —I can't get over the fact that you were born a thousand years ago, Kenri Shaun. That you will still be traveling between the stars when I am down in dust."

It was an obvious opening for a compliment, but his tongue was locked with awkwardness. He was a space farer, a Kithman, a dirty slimy tommy, and she was Star-Free, unspecialized genius, the finest flower of the Empire's genetic hierarchy. He said only: "It is no paradox, Freelady. As the relative velocity approaches that of light, the measured time interval decreases, just as the mass increases; but only to a 'stationary' observer. One set of measurements is as 'real' as another. We're running with a tau factor of *about 33 this trip, which means that it takes us some four months to go from Sirius to Sol; but to a watcher at either star, we'll take almost eleven years."* His mouth felt stiff, but he twisted it into a smile. *"That's not so long, Freelady. You'll have been gone, let's see, twice eleven plus a year in the Sirian System—twenty-four years. Your estates will still be there."*

"Doesn't it take an awful reaction mass?" she asked. *A fine line appeared on the broad forehead as she frowned, trying to understand.*

"No, Freelady. Or, rather, it does, but we don't have to expel matter as an interplanetary ship must. The field drive reacts directly against the mass of local stars—theoretically the entire universe—and converts our mercury 'ballast' into kinetic energy for the rest of the ship. It acts equally on all mass, so we don't experience acceleration pressure and can approach light speed in a few days. In fact, if we didn't rotate the ship, we'd be weightless. When we reach Sol, the agoratron will convert the energy back into mercury atoms and we'll again be almost stationary with respect to Earth."

"I'm afraid I never was much good at physics," she laughed. *"We leave that to Star-A and Norm-A types on Earth."*

The sense of rejection was strangling in him. Yes, *he thought*, brain work and muscle work are still just work. Let the inferiors sweat over it, Star-Frees need all their time just to be ornamental. *Her fingers had relaxed, and he drew his hand back to him.*

She looked pained, sensing his hurt, and reached impulsively out to touch his cheek. "I'm sorry," she said quietly. "I didn't mean to . . . I didn't mean what you think."

"It is nothing, Freelady," he said stiffly, to cover his bewilderment. That an aristocrat should apologize—!

"But it is much," she said earnestly. "I know how many people there are who don't like the Kith. You just don't fit into our society, you realize that. You've never really belonged on Earth." A slow flush crept up her pale cheeks, and she looked down. Her lashes were long and smoky black. "But I do know a little about people, Kenri Shaun. I know a superior type when I meet it. You could be a Star-Free yourself, except . . . we might bore you."

"Never that, Freelady," he said thickly.

He had gone away from her with a singing in him. Three months, he thought gloriously, three ship-months yet before they came to Sol.

A hedge rustled dryly as he turned in at the Shaun gate. Overhead, a maple tree stirred, talking to the light wind, and fluttered a blood-colored leaf down on him. *Early frost this year*, he thought. The weather-control system had never been rebuilt after the Mechanoclasts abolished it, and maybe they had been right there. He paused to inhale the smell of the wind. It was cool and damp, full of odors from mould and turned earth and ripened berries. It struck him suddenly that he had never been here during a winter. He had never seen the hills turn white and glittering, or known the immense hush of snowfall.

Warm yellow light spilled out to make circles on

the lawn. He put his hand on the doorplate, it scanned his pattern and the door opened for him. When he walked into the small, cluttered living room, crowded with half a dozen kids, he caught the lingering whiff of dinner and regretted being too late for it. He'd eaten on shipboard, but there was no cook in the Galaxy quite like his mother.

He saluted his parents as custom prescribed, and his father nodded gravely. His mother was less restrained, she hugged him and said how thin he had gotten. The kids said hello and went back to their books and games and chatter. They'd seen their older brother often enough, and were too young to realize what his decision of resigning meant.

"Come, Kenri, I will fix a sandwich for you at least—" said his mother. "It is good to have you back."

"I haven't time," he said. Helplessly: "I'd like to, but—well—I have to go out again."

She turned away. "Theye Barinn was asking about you," she said, elaborately casual. "The *High Barbaree* got back an Earth-month ago."

"Oh, yes," he said. "I met her on the street."

"Theye is a nice girl," said his mother. "You ought to go call on her. It's not too late tonight."

"Some other time," he said.

"The *High Barbaree* is off to Tau Ceti in another two months," said his mother. "You won't have much chance to see Theye, unless—" Her voice trailed off. *Unless you marry her. She's your sort, Kenri. She would belong well on the* Fleetwing. *She would give me strong grandchildren.*

"Some other time," he repeated. He regretted the

brusqueness in his tone, but he couldn't help it. Turning to his father: "Dad, what's this about a new tax on us?"

Volden Shaun scowled. "A damned imposition," he said. "May all their spacesuits spring leaks. We have to wear these badges now, and pay through the nose for them."

"Can . . . can I borrow yours for tonight? I have to go into the city."

Slowly, Volden met the eyes of his son. Then he sighed and got up. "It's in my study," he said. "Come along and help me find it."

They entered the little room together. It was filled with Volden's books—he read on every imaginable subjects, like most Kithmen—and his carefully polished astrogation instruments and his mementos of other voyages. It all meant something. That intricately chased sword had been given him by an armorer on Procyon V, a many-armed monster who had been his friend. That stereograph was a view of the sharp hills on Isis, frozen gases like molten amber in the glow of mighty Osiris. That set of antlers was from a hunting trip on Loki, in the days of his youth. That light, leaping statuette had been a god on Dagon. Volden's close-cropped gray head bent over the desk, his hands fumbling among the papers.

"Do you really mean to go through with this resignation?" he asked quietly.

Kenri's face grew warm. "Yes," he said. "I'm sorry, but—Yes."

"I've seen others do it," said Volden. "They even prospered, most of them. But I don't think they were ever very happy."

"I wonder," said Kenri.

"The *Fleetwing*'s next trip will probably be clear to Rigel," said Volden. "We won't be back for more than a thousand years. There won't be any Star Empire here. Your very name will be forgotten."

"I heard talk about that voyage." Kenri's voice thickened a little. "It's one reason I'm staying behind."

Volden looked up, challengingly. "What's so good about the Stars?" he asked. "I've seen twelve hundred years of human history, good times and bad times. This is not one of the good times. And it's going to get worse."

Kenri didn't answer.

"That girl is out of your class, son," said Volden. "She's a Star-Free. You're just a damn filthy tommy."

"The prejudice against us isn't racial," said Kenri, avoiding his father's gaze. "It's cultural. A spaceman who goes terrestrial is . . . all right by them."

"So far," said Volden. "It's beginning to get racial already, though. We may all have to abandon Earth for a while."

"I'll get into her class," said Kenri. "Give me that badge."

Volden sighed. "We'll have to overhaul the ship to raise our tau factor," he said. "You've got a good six months yet. We won't leave any sooner. I hope you'll change your mind."

"I might," said Kenri, and knew he lied in his teeth.

"Here it is." Volden held out a small yellow loop of braided cords. "Pin it on your jacket." He took forth a heavy wallet. "And here is a thousand decards of your money. You've got fifty thousand more in the bank, but don't let this get stolen."

Kenri fastened the symbol on. It seemed to have weight, like a stone around his neck. He was saved from deeper humiliation by the automatic reaction of his mind. Fifty thousand decards . . . what to buy? A spaceman necessarily invested in tangible and lasting property—

Then he remembered that he would be staying here. The money ought to have value during his lifetime, at least. And money had a way of greasing the skids of prejudice.

"I'll be back . . . tomorrow, maybe," he said. "Thanks, Dad. Goodnight."

Volden's gaunt face drew into tighter lines. His voice was toneless, but it caught just a little.

"Goodnight, son," he said.

Kenri went out the door, into the darkness of Earth.

The first time, neither of them had been much impressed. Captain Seralpin had told Kenri: "We've got us another passenger. She's over at Landfall, on Ishtar. Want to pick her up?"

"Let her stay there till we're ready to leave," said Kenri. "Why would she want to spend a month on Marduk?"

Seralpin shrugged: "I don't know or care. But she'll pay for conveyance here. Take Boat Five," he said.

Kenri had fueled up the little interplanetary flitter

and shot away from the Fleetwing, *grumbling to himself. Ishtar was on the other side of Sirius at the moment, and even on an acceleration orbit it took days to get there. He spent the time studying Murinn's* General Cosmology, *a book he'd never gotten around to before though it was a good 2500 years old. There had been no basic advance in science since the fall of the African Empire, he reflected, and on Earth today the conviction was that all the important questions had been answered. After all, the universe was finite, so the scientific horizon must be too; after several hundred years during which research turned up no phenomenon not already predicted by theory, there would naturally be a loss of interest which ultimately became a dogma.*

Kenri wasn't sure the dogma was right. He had seen too much of the cosmos to have any great faith in man's ability to understand it. There were problems in a hundred fields — physics, chemistry, biology, psychology, history, epistemology — to which the Nine Books gave no quantitative answer; but when he tried to tell an Earthling that, he got a blank look or a superior smile . . . . No, science was a social enterprise, it couldn't exist when the society didn't want it. But no civilization lasts forever. Someday there would again be a questioning.

Most of the Fleetwing's *passengers were time-expired engineers or planters returning home. Few of the big ships had ever transported a Star aristocrat. When he came down to Landfall, in a spuming rain, and walked through the hot wet streets and onto the bowered verandah of the town's hostel, it was a shock to find that his cargo was a young and beautiful*

*woman. He bowed to her, crossing arms on breast as
prescribed, and felt the stiffness of embarrassment.
He was the outsider, the inferior, the space tramp,
and she was one of Earth's owners.*

*"I hope the boat will not be too uncomfortable for
you, Freelady," he mumbled, and hated himself for
the obsequiousness of it. He should have said, you
useless brainless bitch, my people keep Earth alive
and you ought to be kneeling to me in thanks. But he
bowed again instead, and helped her up the ladder
into the cramped cabin.*

*"I'll make out," she laughed. She was too young,
he guessed, to have taken on the snotty manners of
her class. The fog of Ishtar lay in cool drops in her
hair, like small jewels. The blue eyes were not un-
friendly as they rested on his sharp dark face.*

*He computed an orbit back to Marduk. "It'll take
us four-plus days, Freelady," he said. "I hope you
aren't in too much of a hurry."*

*"Oh, no," she said. "I just wanted to see that
planet too, before leaving." He thought of what it
must be costing her, and felt a vague sense of outrage
that anyone should throw good money around on
mere tourism; but he only nodded.*

*They were in space before long. He emerged from
his curtained bunk after a few hours' sleep to find her
already up, leafing through Murinn. "I don't understand a word of it," she said. "Does he ever use one
syllable where six will do?"*

*"He cared a great deal for precision, Freelady,"
said Kenri as he started breakfast. Impulsively, he
added: "I would have liked to know him."*

Her eyes wandered around the boat's library, shelf

on shelf of microbooks and full-sized volumes. "You people do a lot of reading, don't you?" she asked.

"Not too much else to do on a long voyage, Freelady," he said. "There are handicrafts, of course, and the preparation of goods for sale—things like that—but there's still plenty of time for reading."

"I'm surprised you have such big crews," she said. "Surely you don't need that many people to man a ship."

"No, Freelady," he replied. "A ship between the stars just about runs herself. But when we reach a planet, a lot of hands are needed."

"There's company too, I suppose," she ventured. "Wives and children and friends."

"Yes, Freelady." His voice grew cold. What business of hers was it?

"I like your Town," she said. "I used to go there often. It's so—quaint? Like a bit of the past, kept alive all these centuries."

Sure, he wanted to say, sure, your sort come around to stare. You come around drunk, and peer into our homes, and when an old man goes by you remark what a funny little geezer he is, without even lowering your voices, and when you bargain with a shopkeeper and he tries to get a fair price it only proves to you that all tommies think of nothing but money. Oh, yes, we're very glad to have you visit us. "Yes, Freelady."

She looked hurt, and said little for many hours. After a while she went back into the space he had screened off for her, and he heard her playing a violin. It was a very old melody, older than man's starward wish, unbelievably old, and still it was *young and tender and trustful, still it was everything which was good and dear in man. He couldn't quite track down the music, what was it—? After a while, she stopped. He felt a desire to impress her. The Kith had their own tunes. He got out his guitar and strummed a few chords and let his mind wander.*

Presently he began to sing.

"When Jerry Clawson was a baby
On his mother's knee in old Kentuck,
He said: 'I'm gonna ride those deep-space
   rockets
Till the bones in my body turn to dust.'—"

He sensed her come quietly out and stand behind him, but pretended not to be aware of her. His voice lilted between the thrumming walls, and he looked out toward cold stars and the ruddy crescent of Marduk.

"—Jerry's voice came o'er the speaker:
'Cut your cable and go free.
On full thrust, she's blown more shielding.
Radiation's got to me.

'Take the boats in safety Earthward.
Tell the Fireball Line for me
I was born to ride through deep space,
Now in deep space forevermore I'll be.' "

He ended it with a crash of strings and looked around and got up to bow.

"No . . . sit down," *she said.* "This isn't Earth.

What was that song?''

*"Jerry Clawson, Freelady,'' he replied. "It's an-
cient—in fact, I was singing a translation from the
original English. It goes clear back to the early days of
interplanetary travel.''*

*Star-Frees were supposed to be intellectuals as well
as esthetes. He waited for her to say that somebody
ought to collect Kith folk ballads in a book.*

"I like it,'' she said. "I like it very much.''

*He looked away. "Thank you, Freelady,'' he said.
"May I make bold to ask what you were playing
earlier?''*

*"Oh . . . that's even older,'' she said. "A theme
from the* Kreutzer Sonata. *I'm awfully fond of it.''
She smiled slowly. "I think I would have liked to
know Beethoven.''*

*They met each other's eyes, then, and did not look
away or speak for what seemed like a long time.*

The Town ended as sharply as if cut off by a knife.
It had been like that for 3000 years, a sanctuary from
time: sometimes it stood alone on open windy moors,
with no other work of man in sight except a few
broken walls; sometimes it was altogether swallowed
by a roaring monster of a city; sometimes, as now, it
lay on the fringe of a great commune; but always it
was the Town, changeless and inviolate.

No—not so. There had been days when war swept
through it, pockmarking walls and sundering roofs
and filling its streets with corpses; there had been
murderous mobs looking for a tommy to lynch; there
had been haughty swaggering officers come to

enforce some new proclamation. They could return. Through all the endless turmoil of history, they would. Kenri shivered in the wandering autumn breeze and started off along the nearest avenue.

The neighborhood was a slum at the moment, gaunt crumbling tenements, cheerless lanes, aimlessly drifting crowds. They wore doublets and kilts of sleazy gray, and they stank. Most of them were Norms, nominally free—which meant free to starve when there wasn't work to be had. The majority were Norm-Ds, low-class manual laborers with dull heavy faces, but here and there the more alert countenance of a Norm-C or B showed briefly in the glare of a lamp, above the weaving, sliding shadows. When a Standard pushed through, gay in the livery of the state or his private owner, something flickered in those eyes. A growing knowledge, a feeling that something was wrong when slaves were better off than freemen—Kenri had seen that look before, and knew what it could become: the blind face of destruction. And elsewhere were the men of Mars and Venus and the Jovian moons, yes, the Radiant of Jupiter had ambitions and Earth was still the richest planet . . . No, he thought, the Star Empire wouldn't last much longer.

But it ought to last his and Dorthy's lifetime, and they could make some provision for their children. That was enough.

An elbow jarred into his ribs. "Outta the way, tommy!"

He clenched his fists, thinking of what he had done beyond the sky, what he could do here on Earth —Silently, he stepped off the walk. A woman, leaning fat and blowsy from an upstairs window, jeered at him and spat. He dodged the fleck of spittle, but he could not dodge the laughter that followed him.

They hate, he thought. *They still don't dare resent their masters, so they take it out on us. Be patient. It cannot endure another two centuries.*

It still shook in him, though. He grew aware of the tautness in his nerves and belly, and his neck ached with the strain of keeping his face humbly lowered. Though Dorthy was waiting for him in a garden of roses, he needed a drink. He saw the winking neon bottle and turned in that door.

A few sullen men were slumped at tables, under the jerky obscenity of a live mural that must be a hundred years old. The tavern owned only half a dozen Standard-D girls, and they were raddled things who must have been bought third hand. One of them gave Kenri a mechanical smile, saw his face and dress and badge, and turned away with a sniff.

He made his way to the bar. There was a live tender who showed him a glazed stare. "Vodzan," said Kenri. "Make it a double."

"We don't serve no tommies here," said the bartender.

Kenri's fingers whitened on the bar. He turned to go, but a hand touched his arm. "Just a minute, spaceman." To the attendant: "One double vodzan."

"I told you—"

"This is for me, Wilm. And I can give it to anyone I want. I can pour it on the floor if I so desire." There was a thinness in the tone, and the bartender went quickly off to his bottles.

Kenri looked into a white, hairless face with a rakish cast to its skull structure. The lean gray-clad body was hunched over the bar, one hand idly rolling dice from a cup. There were no bones in the fingers, they were small delicate tentacles; and the eyes were colored like ruby.

"Thank you," said Kenri. "May I pay—"

"No. It's on me." The other accepted the glass and handed it over. "Here."

"Your health, sir." Kenri lifted the glass and drank. The liquor was pungent fire along his throat.

"Such as it is," said the man indifferently. "No trouble to me. What I say here goes." He was probably a petty criminal of some sort, perhaps a member of the now outlawed Assassins' Guild. And the body type was not quite human. He must be a Special-X, created in the genetic labs for a particular job or for study or for amusement. Presumably he had been set free when his owner was done with him, and had made a place for himself in the slums.

"Been gone long?" he asked, looking at the dice.

"About twenty-three years," said Kenri. "Sirius."

"Things have changed," said the X. "Anti-Kithism is growing strong again. Be careful you aren't slugged or robbed, because if you are, it'll do you no good to appeal to the city guards."

"It's nice of you to—"

"Nothing." The slim fingers scooped up the dice and rattled the cup again. "I like somebody to feel superior to."

"Oh." Kenri set the glass down. For a moment, the smoky room blurred. "I see. Well—"

"No, don't go off." The ruby eyes lifted up to his, and he was surprised to see tears in them. "I'm sorry. You can't blame me for being bitter. I wanted to sign on myself, once, and they wouldn't have me."

Kenri said nothing.

"I would, of course, give my left leg to the breast-bone for a chance to go on just one voyage," said the X dully. "Don't you think an Earthling has his dreams now and then—we too? But I wouldn't be much use. You have to grow up in space, damn near, to know enough to be of value on some planet Earth never heard of. And I suppose there's my looks too. Even the underdogs can't get together any more."

"They never could, sir," said Kenri.

"I suppose you're right. You've seen more of both space and time than I ever will. So I stay here, belonging nowhere, and keep alive somehow; but I wonder if it's worth the trouble. A man isn't really alive till he has something bigger than himself and his own little happiness, for which he'd gladly die. Oh, well." The X rolled out the dice. "Nine. I'm losing my touch." Glancing up again: "I know a place where they don't care who you are if you've got money."

"Thank you, sir, but I have business elsewhere," said Kenri awkwardly.

"I thought so. Well, go ahead, then. Don't let me stop you." The X looked away.

"Thank you for the drink, sir."

"It was nothing. Come in whenever you want, I'm usually here. But don't yarn to me about the planets out there. I don't want to hear that."

"Goodnight," said Kenri.

As he walked out, the dice clattered across the bar again.

Dorthy had wanted to do some surface traveling on Marduk, get to see the planet. She could have had her pick of the colony for escorts, but she chose to ask Kenri. One did not say no to a Star, so he dropped some promising negotiations for pelts with a native chief, hired a groundcar, and picked her up at the time she set.

They rode quietly for a while, until the settlement was lost behind the horizon. Here was stony desert, flamboyantly colored, naked crags and iron hills and low dusty thorn-trees sharp in the thin clear air. Overhead, the sky was a royal blue, with the shrunken disc of Sirius A and the brilliant spark of its companion spilling harsh light over the stillness.

"This is a beautiful world," she said at last. Her tones came muffled through the tenuous air. "I like it better than Ishtar."

"Most people don't, Freelady," he answered. "They call it dull and cold and dry."

"They don't know," she said. Her fair head was turned from him, looking at the fantastic loom of a nearby scarp, gnawed rocks and straggling brush, tawny color streaked with the blue and red lightning of mineral veins.

"I envy you, Kenri Shaun," she said at last. "I've seen a few pictures, read a few books—everything I could get hold of, but it isn't enough. When I think of all you have seen that is strange and beautiful and wonderful, I envy you."

He ventured a question: "Was that why you came to Sirius, Freelady?"

"In part. When my father died, we wanted someone to check on the family's Ishtarian holdings. Everyone assumed we'd just send an agent, but I insisted on going myself, and booked with the Temeraire. They all thought I was crazy. Why, I'd come back to new styles, new slang, new people . . . my friends would all be middle-aged, I'd be a walking anachronism . . . you know." She sighed. "But it was worth it."

He thought of his own life, the grinding sameness of the voyages, weeks slipping into months and years within a pulsing metal shell; approach, strangeness, the savage hostility of cruel planets—he had seen friends buried under landslides, spitting out their lungs when helmets cracked open in airlessness, rotting alive with some alien sickness; he had told them goodbye and watched them go off into a silence which never gave them back and had wondered how they came to die; and on Earth he was a ghost, not belonging, adrift above the great river of time, on Earth he felt somehow unreal. "I wonder, Freelady," he said.

"Oh, I'll adjust," she laughed.

The car ground its way over high dunes and down tumbling ravines, it left a track in the dust which the slow wind erased behind them. That night they camped near the ruins of a forgotten city, a place which must once have been a faerie spectacle of loveliness. Kenri set up the two tents and started a meal on the glower while she watched. "Let me help," she offered once.

"It isn't fitting, Freelady," he replied. And you'd be too clumsy anyway, you'd only make a mess of it. *His hands were deft on the primitive skillet. The ruddy light of the glower beat against darkness, etching their faces red in windy shadows. Overhead, the stars were high and cold.*

She looked at the sputtering meal. "I thought you . . . people never ate fish," she murmured.

"Some of us do, some don't, Freelady," he said absently. *Out here, it was hard to resent the gulf between them.* *"It was originally tabooed by custom in the Kith back when space and energy for growing food on shipboard were at a premium. Only a rich man could have afforded an aquarium, you see; and a tight-knit group of nomads has to ban conspicuous consumption to prevent ill feeling. Nowadays, when the economic reason has long disappeared, only the older people still observe the taboo."*

She smiled, accepting the plate he handed her. *"It's funny,"* she said. *"One just doesn't think of your people as having a history. You've always been around."*

"Oh, we do, Freelady. We've plenty of traditions than the rest of mankind, perhaps."

A hunting marcat screamed in the night. She shivered. "What's that?"

"Local carnivore, Freelady. Don't let it worry you." He slapped his slug-thrower, obscurely pleased at a chance to show—what? Manliness? *"No one with a weapon has to fear any larger animals. It's other things that make the danger—occasionally a disease, more often cold or heat or poison gases or vacuum or whatever hell the universe can brew for*

us." He grinned, a flash of teeth in the dark lean face. "Anyway, if it ate us it would die pretty quickly. We're as poisonous to it as it is to us."

"Different biochemistry and ecology," she nodded. "A billion or more years of separate evolution. It would be strange, wouldn't it, if more than a very few planets had developed life so close to Earth's that we could eat it. I suppose that's why there never was any real extrasolar colonization—just a few settlements for mining or trading or extracting organic chemicals."

"That's partly it, Freelady," he said. "Matter of economics, too. It was much easier—in money terms, cheaper—for people to stay at home; no significant percentage of them could ever have been taken away in any event—human breeding would have raised the population faster than emigration could lower it."

She gave him a steady look. When she spoke, her voice was soft. "You Kithmen are a brainy lot, aren't you?"

He knew it was true, but he made the expected disclaimer.

"No, no," she said. "I've read up on your history a little. Correct me if I'm wrong, but since the earliest times of space travel the qualifications have been pretty rigid. A spaceman just had to be of high intelligence, with quick reactions and stable personality both. And he couldn't be too large, physically; but he had to be tough. And a dark complexion must be of some small help, now and then, in strong sunlight or radiation . . . . Yes, that was how it was. How it still is. When women began going to space too, the trade naturally tended to run in families.

Those spacemen who didn't fit into the life, dropped out; and the recruits from Sol were pretty similar in mind and body to the people they joined. So eventually you got the Kith—almost a separate race of man; and it evolved its own ways of living. Until at last you had a monopoly on space traffic.''

"No, Freelady," he said. "We've never had that. Anyone who wants to build a spaceship and man it himself, can do so. But it's an enormous capital investment; and after the initial glamour had worn off, the average Solarian just wasn't interested in a hard and lonely life. So today, all spacemen are Kithmen, but it was never planned that way."

"That's what I meant," she said. Earnestly. "And your being different naturally brought suspicion and discrimination . . . . No, don't interrupt, I want to say this through . . . . Any conspicuous minority which offers competition to the majority is going to be disliked. Sol has to have the fissionables you bring from the stars, we've used up our own; and the unearthly chemicals you bring are often of great value, and the trade in luxuries like furs and jewels is brisk. So you are essential to society, but you still don't really belong in it. You are too proud, in your own way, to ape your oppressors. Being human, you naturally charge all the traffic will bear, which gives you the reputation of being gougers; being able to think better and faster than the average Solarian, you can usually best him in a deal, and he hates you for it. Then there's the tradition handed down from Mechanoclastic times, when technology was considered evil and only you maintained a high level of it. And in the puritan stage of the Martian conquest, your cus-

tom of wife trading—oh, I know you do it just to relieve the endless monotony of the voyages, I know you have more family life than we do—Well, all those times are gone, but they've left their legacy. I wonder why you bother with Earth at all. Why you don't all just wander into space and let us stew in our own juice.''

''Earth is our planet too, Freelady,'' he said, very quietly. After a moment: *''The fact that we are essential gives us some protection. We get by. Please don't feel sorry for us.''*

''A stiff-necked people,'' she said. *''You don't even want pity.''*

''Who does, Freelady?'' he asked.

On the edge of the slum, in a zone bulking with the tall warehouses and offices of the merchant families, Kenri took an elevator up to the public skyway going toward the address he wanted. There was no one else in sight at that point; he found a seat and lowered himself into it and let the strip hum him toward city center.

The skyway climbed fast, until he was above all but the highest towers. Leaning an arm on the rail, he looked down into a night that was alive with radiance. The streets and walls glowed, strings of colored lamps flashed and flashed against a velvet dark, fountains leaped white and gold and scarlet, a flame display danced like molten rainbows at the feet of a triumphal statue. Star architecture was a thing of frozen motion, soaring columns and tiers and pinnacles to challenge the burning sky; high in that airy jungle, the spaceman could hardly make out the river of vehicles and humanity below him.

As he neared the middle of town, the skyway gathered more passengers. Standards in bright fantastic livery, Norms in their tunics and kilts, an occasional visitor from Mars or Venus or Jupiter with resplendent uniform and greedy smoldering eyes—yes, and here came a party of Frees, their thin garments, a swirling iridescence about the erect slender forms, a hard glitter of jewels, the men's beards and the women's hair elaborately curled. Fashions had changed in the past two decades. Kenri felt acutely aware of his own shabbiness, and huddled closer to the edge of the strip.

Two young couples passed his seat. He caught a woman's voice: "Oh, look, a tommy!"

"He's got a nerve," mumbled one of the men. "I've half a mind to—"

"No, Scanish." Another feminine voice, gentler than the first. "He has the right."

"He shouldn't have. I know these tommies. Give 'em a finger and they'll take your whole arm." The four were settling into the seat behind Kenri's. "My uncle is in Transsolar Trading. He'll tell you."

"Please, no, Scanish, he's listening!"

"And I hope he—"

"Never mind, dear. What shall we do next? Go to Halgor's?" She attempted a show of interest.

"Ah, we've been there a hundred times. What is there to do? How about getting my rocket and shooting over to China? I know a place where they got techniques you never—"

"No. I'm not in the mood. I don't know what I

want to do.''

"My nerves have been terrible lately. We bought a new doctor, but he says just the same as the old one. They don't any of them know which end is up. I might try this new Beltanist religion, they seem to have something. It would at least be amusing.''

"Say, have you heard about Marla's latest? You know who was seen coming out of her bedroom last ten-day?''

Kenri grabbed hold of his mind and forced it away from listening. He didn't want to. He wouldn't let the weariness and sickness of spirit which was the old tired Empire invade him.

Dorthy, he thought. *Dorthy Persis from Canda. It's a beautiful name, isn't it? There's music in it. And the from Candas have always been an outstanding family. She isn't like the rest of the Stars.*

She loves me, he thought with a singing in him. *She loves me. There is a life before us. Two of us, one life, and the rest of the Empire can rot as it will. We'll be together.*

He saw the skyscraper ahead of him now, a thing of stone and crystal and light that climbed toward heaven in one great rush. The insigne of the from Candas burned on its façade, an ancient and proud symbol. It stood for 300 years of achievement.

But that's less than my own lifetime. No, I don't have to be ashamed in their presence. I come of the oldest and best line of all humanity. I'll fit in.

He wondered why he could not shake off the depression that clouded him. This was a moment of glory. He should be going to her as a conqueror. But—

He sighed and rose as his stop approached.

Pain stabbed at him. He jumped, stumbled, and fell to one knee. Slowly, his head twisted around. The young Star grinned in his face, holding up a shockstick. Kenri's hand rubbed the pain, and the four people began to laugh. So did everyone else in sight. The laughter followed him off the skyway and down to the ground.

There was no one else on the bridge. One man was plenty to stand watch, here in the huge emptiness between suns. The room was a hollow cavern of twilight, quiet except for the endless throbbing of the ship. Here and there, the muted light of instrument panels glowed, and the weird radiance of the distorted stars flamed in the viewport. But otherwise there was no illumination, Kenri had switched it off.

She came through the door and paused, her gown white in the dusk. His throat tightened as he looked at her, and when he bowed, his head swam. There was a faint sweet rustling as she walked closer. She had the long swinging stride of freedom, and her unbound hair floated silkily behind her.

"I've never been on a bridge before," she said. "I didn't think passengers were allowed there."

"I invited you, Freelady," he answered, his voice catching.

"It was good of you, Kenri Shaun." Her fingers fluttered across his arm. "You have always been good to me."

"Could anyone be anything else, to you?" he asked.

Light stole along her cheeks and into the eyes that turned up at his. She smiled with a strangely timid curve of lips. "Thank you," she whispered.

"Ah, I, well—" He gestured at the viewport, which seemed to hang above their heads. "That is precisely on the ship's axis of rotation, Freelady," he said. "That's why the view is constant. Naturally, 'down' on the bridge is any point at which you are standing. You'll note that the desks and panels are arranged in a circle around the inner wall, to take advantage of that fact." His voice sounded remote and strange to his ears. "Now here we have the astrogation computer. Ours is badly in need of overhauling just now, which is why you see all those books and calculations on my desk—"

Her hand brushed the back of his chair. "This is yours, Kenri Shaun? I can almost see you working away on it, with that funny tight look on your face, as if the problem were your personal enemy. Then you sigh, and run your fingers through your hair, and put your feet on the desk to think for a while. Am I right?"

"How did you guess, Freelady?"

"I know. I've thought a great deal about you, lately." She looked away, out to the harsh blue-white stars clustered in the viewport.

Suddenly her fists gathered themselves. "I wish you didn't make me feel so futile," she said.

"You—"

"This is life, here." She spoke swiftly, blurring the words in her need to say them. "You're keeping Earth alive, with your cargoes. You're working and fighting and thinking about—about something real.

Not about what to wear for dinner and who was seen where with whom and what to do tonight when you're too restless and unhappy to stay quietly at home. You're keeping Earth alive, I said, and a dream too. I envy you, Kenri Shaun. I wish I were born into the Kith."

"Freelady—" It rattled in his throat.

"No use." She smiled, without self-pity. "Even if a ship would have me, I could never go. I don't have the training, or the inborn strength, or the patience, or—No! Forget it." There were tears in the ardent eyes. "When I get home, knowing now what you are in the Kith, will I even try to help you? Will I work for more understanding of your people, kindness, common decency? No. I'll realize it's useless even to try. I won't have the courage."

"You'd be wasting your time, Freelady," he said. "No one person can change a whole culture. Don't worry about it."

"I know," she replied. "You're right, of course. You're always right. But in my place, you would try!"

They stared at each other for a long moment.

That was the first time he kissed her.

The two guards at the soaring main entrance were giants, immobile as statues in the sunburst glory of their uniforms. Kenri had to crane his neck to look into the face of the nearest. "The Freelady Dorthy Persis is expecting me," he said.

"Huh?" Shock brought the massive jaw clicking down.

"That's right." Kenri grinned and extended the card she had given him. "She said to look her up immediately."

"But—there's a party going on—"

"Never mind. Call her up."

The guardsman reddened, opened his mouth, and snapped it shut again. Turning, he went to the visiphone booth. Kenri waited, regretting his insolence. *Give 'em a finger and they'll take your whole arm.* But how else could a Kithman behave? If he gave deference, they called him a servile bootlicker; if he showed his pride, he was an obnoxious pushing bastard; if he dickered for a fair price, he was a squeezer and bloodsucker; if he spoke his own old language to his comrades, he was being secretive; if he cared more for his skyfaring people than for an ephemeral nation, he was a traitor and coward; if—

The guard returned, shaking his head in astonishment. "All right," he said sullenly. "Go on up. First elevator to your right, fiftieth floor. But watch your manners, tommy."

When I'm adopted into the masters, thought Kenri savagely, *I'll make him eat that word.* Then, with a new rising of the unaccountable weariness: *No. Why should I? What would anyone gain by it?*

He went under the enormous curve of the door, into a foyer that was a grotto of luminous plastic. A few Standard servants goggled at him, but made no move to interfere. He found the elevator cage and punched for 50. It rose in a stillness broken only by the sudden rapid thunder of his heart.

He emerged into an anteroom of red velvet. Beyond an arched doorway, he glimpsed colors floating, a human blaze of red and purple and gold; the air was loud with music and laughter. The footman at the entrance stepped in his path, hardly believing the sight. "You can't go in there!"

"The hell I can't." Kenri shoved him aside and strode through the arch. The radiance hit him like a fist, and he stood blinking at the confusion of dancers, servants, onlookers, entertainers—there must be a thousand people in the vaulted chamber.

"Kenri! Oh, Kenri—"

She was in his arms, pressing her mouth to his, drawing his head down with shaking hands. He strained her close, and the misty cloak she wore whirled about to wrap them in aloneness.

One moment, and then she drew back breathlessly, laughing a little. It wasn't quite the merriment he had known, there was a thin note to it, and shadows lay under the great eyes. She was very tired, he saw, and pity lifted in him. "Dearest," he whispered.

"Kenri, not here . . . Oh, darling, I hoped you would come sooner, but—No, come with me now, I want them all to see the man I've got with me." She took his hand and half dragged him forward. The dancers were stopping, pair by pair as they noticed the stranger, until at last there were a thousand faces stiffly turned to his. Silence dropped like a thunderclap, but the music kept on. It sounded tinny in the sudden quiet.

Dorthy shivered. Then she threw back her head with a defiance that was dear to him and met the eyes. Her arm rose to bring the wristphone to her lips, and the ceiling amplifiers boomed her voice over the room: "Friends, I want to announce . . . Some of you already know . . . well, this is the man I'm going to marry—"

It was the voice of a frightened little girl. Cruel to make it loud as a goddess talking.

After a pause which seemed to last forever, somebody performed the ritual bow. Then somebody else did, and then they were all doing it, like jointed dolls. There were a few scornful exceptions, who turned their backs.

"Go on!" Dorthy's tones grew shrill. "Go on dancing. Please! You'll all—later—" The orchestra leader must have had a degree of sensitivity, for he struck up a noisy tune and one by one the couples slipped into a figure dance.

Dorothy looked hollowly up at the spaceman. "It's good to see you again," she said.

"And you," he replied.

"Come." She led him around the wall. "Let's sit and talk."

They found an alcove, screened from the room by a trellis of climbing roses. It was a place of dusk, and she turned hungrily to him. He felt how she trembled.

"It hasn't been easy for you, has it?" he asked tonelessly.

"No," she said.

"If you—"

"Don't say it!" There was fear in the words. She closed his mouth with hers.

"I love you," she said after a while. "That's all that matters, isn't it?"

He didn't answer.

"Isn't it?" she cried.

He nodded. "Maybe. I take it your family and friends don't approve of your choice."

"Some don't. Does it matter, darling? They'll forget, when you're one of us."

"One of you—I'm not born to this," he said bleakly. "I'll always stick out like—Well, never mind. I can stand it if you can."

He sat on the padded bench, holding her close, and looked out through the clustered blooms. Color and motion and high harsh laughter—it wasn't his world. He wondered why he had ever assumed it could become his.

They had talked it out while the ship plunged through night. She could never be of the Kith. There was no room in a crew for one who couldn't endure worlds never meant for man. He would have to join her instead. He could fit in, he had the intelligence and adaptability to make a place for himself.

What kind of place? he wondered as she nestled against him. A planner of more elaborate parties, a purveyor of trivial gossip, a polite ear for boredom and stupidity and cruelty and perversion—No, there would be Dorthy, they would be alone in the nights of Earth and that would be enough.

Would it? A man couldn't spend all his time making love.

There were the big trading firms, he could go far in one of them. (Four thousand barrels of Kalian jung oil rec'd. pr. acct., and the fierce rains and lightning across the planet's phosphorescent seas. A thousand refined thorium ingots from Hathor, and moonlight sparkling the crisp snow and the ringing winter stillness. A bale of green furs from a newly discovered planet, and the ship had gone racing through stars and splendor into skies no man had ever seen.) Or perhaps the military. (Up on your feet, soldier! Hup, hup, hup, hup!. . . Sir, the latest Intelligence report on Mars . . . Sir, I know the guns aren't up to spec, but we can't touch the contractor, his patron is a Star-Free . . . . The General commands your presence at a banquet for staff officers . . . . Now tell me, Colonel Shaun, tell me what you *really* think will happen, you officers are all so *frightfully* close-mouthed . . . . Ready! Aim! Fire! So perish all traitors to the Empire!) Or even the science centers. (Well, sir, according to the book, the formula is . . .)

Kenri's arm tightened desperately about Dorthy's waist.

"How do you like being home?" he asked. "Otherwise, I mean."

"Oh—fine. Wonderful!" She smiled uncertainly at him. "I was so afraid I'd be old-fashioned, out of touch, but no, I fell in right away. There's the most terribly amusing crowd, a lot of them children of my own old crowd. You'll love them, Kenri. I have a lot of glamour, you know, for going clear to Sirius. Think how much you'll have!"

"I won't," he grunted. "I'm just a tommy, remember?"

"Kenri!" Anger flicked across her brow. "What a way to talk. You aren't, and you know it, and you won't be unless you insist on thinking like one all the time—" She caught herself and said humbly: "I'm sorry, darling. That was a terrible thing to say, wasn't it?"

He stared ahead of him.

"I've been, well, infected," she said. "You were gone so long. You'll cure me again."

Tenderness filled him, and he kissed her.

"A-hum! Pardon!"

They jerked apart, almost guiltily, and looked up to the two who had entered the alcove. One was a middle-aged man, austerely slender and erect, his night-blue tunic flashing with decorations; the other was younger, pudgy-faced, and rather drunk. Kenri got up. He bowed with his arms straight, as one equal to another.

"Oh, you must meet, I know you'll like each other—" Dorthy was speaking fast, her voice high. "This is Kenri Shaun. I've told you enough about him, haven't I?" A nervous little laugh. "Kenri, my uncle, Colonel from Canda of the Imperial Staff, and my nephew, the Honorable Lord Doms. Fancy coming back and finding you have a nephew your own age!"

"Your honor, sir." The colonel's voice was as stiff as his back. Doms giggled.

"You must pardon the interruption," went on from Canda. "But I wished to speak to . . . to Shaun as soon as possible. You will understand, sir, that it is for the good of my niece and the whole family."

Kenri's palms were cold and wet. "Of course," he said. "Please sit down."

"Thank you." From Canda lowered his angular frame onto the bench, next to the Kithman; Doms and Dorthy sat at opposite ends, the young man slumped over and grinning. "Shall I send for some wine?"

"Not for me, thanks," said Kenri huskily.

The cold eyes were level on his. "First," said the colonel, "I want you to realize that I do not share this absurd race prejudice which is growing up about your people. It is demonstrable that the Kith is biologically equal to the Star families, and doubtless superior to some." His glance flickered contemptuously over to Doms. "There is a large cultural barrier, of course, but if that can be surmounted, I, for one, would be glad to sponsor your adoption into our ranks."

"Thank you, sir." Kenri felt dizzy. No Kithman had ever gone so high in all history. That it should be *him*—! He heard Dorthy's happy little sigh as she took his arm, and something of the frozenness within him began to thaw. "I'll . . . do best—"

"But will you? That is what I have to find out." From Canda leaned forward, clasping his gaunt hands between his knees. "Let us not mince words. You know as well as I that there is a time of great danger ahead for the Empire, and that if it is to survive the few men of action left must stand together and strike hard. We can ill afford the weaklings among us; we can certainly not afford to have strong men in our midst who are not wholeheartedly for our cause."

"I'll be . . . loyal, sir," said Kenri. "What more can I do?"

"Much," said the colonel. "Considerable of it may be distasteful to you. Your special knowledge could be of high value. For example, the new tax on the Kith is not merely a device to humiliate them. We need the money. The Empire's finances are in bad shape, and even that little bit helps. There will have to be further demands, on the Kith as well as everyone else. You can assist us in guiding our policy, so that they are not goaded to the point of abandoning Earth altogether.''

"I—" Kenri swallowed. He felt suddenly ill. "You can't expect—"

"If you won't, then you won't, and I cannot force you," said from Canda. There was a strange brief sympathy in the chill tones. "I am merely warning you of what lies ahead. You could mitigate the lot of your . . . former . . . people considerably, if you help us."

"Why not . . . treat them like human beings?" asked Kenri. "We'll always stand by our friends."

"Three thousand years of history cannot be canceled by decree," said from Canda. "You know that as well as I."

Kenri nodded. It seemed to strain his neck muscles.

"I admire your courage," said the aristocrat. "You have started on a hard road. Can you follow it through?"

Kenri looked down.

"Of course he can," said Dorthy softly.

Lord Doms giggled. "New tax," he said. "Slap a new one on fast. I've got one tommy skipper on the ropes already. Bad voyage, debts, heh!"

Red and black and icy blue, and the shriek of lifting winds.

"Shut up, Doms," said the colonel. "I didn't want you along."

Dorthy's head leaned back against Kenri's shoulder. "Thank you, uncle," she said. There was a lilt in her voice. "If you'll be our friend, it will all work out."

"I hope so," said from Canda.

The faint sweet odor of Dorthy's hair was in Kenri's nostrils. He felt the gold waves brushing his cheek, but still didn't look up. There was thunder and darkness in him.

Doms laughed. "I got to tell you 'bout this spacer," he said. "He owes the firm money, see? I can take his daughter under contract if he doesn't pay up. Only his crew are taking up a collection for him. I got to stop that somehow. They say those tommy girls are mighty hot. How about it, Kenri? You're one of us now. How are they, really? Is it true that—"

Kenri stood up. He saw the room swaying, and wondered dimly if he was wobbling on his feet or not.

"Doms," snapped from Canda, "if you don't shut your mouth—"

Kenri grabbed a handful of Lord Doms' tunic and hauled him to his feet. The other hand became a fist, and the face squashed under it.

He stood over the young man, weaving, his arms hanging loose at his sides. Doms moaned on the floor. Dorthy gave a small scream. From Canda leaped up, clapping his hand to a sidearm.

Kenri lifted his eyes. There was a thickness in his words. "Go ahead and arrest me," he said. "Go on, what are you waiting for?"

"K-k-kenri—" Dorthy touched him with shaking hands.

From Canda grinned and nudged Doms with a boot. "That was foolish of you, Kenri Shaun," he said, "but the job was long overdue. I'll see that nothing happens to you."

"But this Kith girl—"

"She'll be all right too, I daresay, if her father can raise that money." The hard eyes raked Kenri's face. "But remember, my friend, you cannot live in two worlds at once. You are not a Kithman any longer."

Kenri straightened. He knew a sudden dark peace, as if all storms had laid themselves to rest. His head felt a little empty, but utterly clear.

It was a memory in him which had opened his vision and shown him what he must do, the only thing he could do. There was a half-human face and eyes without hope and a voice which had spoken: *"A man isn't really alive till he has something bigger than himself and his own little happiness, for which he'd gladly die."*

"Thank you, sir," he said. "But I am a Kithman. I will always be."

"Kenri—" Dorthy's tone broke. She held his arms and stared at him with wildness.

His hand stroked her hair. "I'm sorry, dearest," he said gently.

"Kenri, you can't go, you can't, you can't—"

"I must," he said. "It was bad enough that I should give up everything which had been my life for an existence that to me is stupid and dreary and meaningless. For you, I could have stood that. But you are asking me to be a tyrant, or at least to be a friend of tyrants. You're asking me to countenance evil. I can't do it. I wouldn't if I could." He took her shoulders and looked into the unseeing bewilderment of her eyes. "Because that would, in the end, make me hate you, who had so twisted my own self, and I want to go on loving you. I will always love you."

She wrenched away from him. He thought that there were psychological treatments to change her feelings and make her stop caring about him. Sooner or later, she'd take one of those. He wanted to kiss her farewell, but he didn't quite dare.

Colonel from Canda extended a hand. "You will be my enemy, I suppose," he said. "But I respect you for it. I like you, and wish—well, good luck to you, Kenri Shaun."

"And to you, sir . . . Goodbye, Dorthy."

He walked through the ballroom, not noticing the eyes that were on him, and out the door to the elevator. He was still too numb to feel anything, that would come later.

Theye Barinn is a nice girl, he thought somewhere on the edge of his mind. *I'll have to go around and see her soon. We could be happy together.*

It seemed like a long while before he was back in the Town. Then he walked along empty streets, alone within himself, breathing the cool damp night wind of Earth.

THE HORN OF TIME THE HUNTER

Now and then, on that planet, Jong Errifrans thought he heard the distant blowing of a horn. It would begin low, with a pulse that quickened as the notes waxed, until the snarl broke in a brazen scream and sank sobbing away. The first time he started and asked the others if they heard. But the sound was on the bare edge of audibility for him, whose ears were young and sharp, and the men said no. "Some trick of the wind, off in the cliffs yonder," Mons Rainart suggested. He shivered. "The damned wind is always hunting here." Jong did not mention it again, but when he heard the noise thereafter a jag of cold went through him.

There was no reason for that. Nothing laired in the city but seabirds, whose wings made a white storm over the tower tops and whose flutings mingled with wind skirl and drum roll of surf; nothing more sinister had appeared than a great tiger-striped fish, which patrolled near the outer reefs. And perhaps that was why Jong feared the horn: it gave the emptiness a voice.

At night, rather than set up their glower, the four would gather wood and give themselves the primitive comfort of a fire. Their camping place was in what might once have been a forum. Blocks of polished stone thrust out of the sand and wiry grass that had occupied all streets; toppled colonnades demarked a square. More shelter was offered by the towers clustered in the city's heart, still piercing the sky, the glasite windows still unbroken. But no, these windows were too much like a dead man's eyes, the rooms within were too hushed, now that the machines that had been the city's life lay corroded beneath the dunes. It was better to raise a tent under the stars. Those, at least, were much the same, after twenty thousand years.

The men would eat, and then Regor Lannis, the leader, would lift his communicator bracelet near his mouth and report their day's ransacking. The spaceboat's radio caught the message and relayed it to the *Golden Flyer*, which orbited with the same period as the planet's twenty-one-hour rotation, so that she was always above this island. "Very little news," Regor typically said. "Remnants of tools and so on. We haven't found any bones yet for a radioactivity dating. I don't think we will, either. They probably cremated their dead, to the very end. Mons has estimated that engine block we found began rusting some ten thousand years ago. He's only guessing, though. It wouldn't have lasted at all if the sand hadn't buried it, and we don't know when that happened.''

"But you say the furnishings inside the towers are mostly intact, age-proof alloys and synthetics,'' answered Captain Ilmaray's voice. ''Can't you deduce anything from their, well, their arrangement or disarrangement? If the city was plundered—''

"No, sir, the signs are too hard to read. A lot of rooms have obviously been stripped. But we don't know whether that was done in one day or over a period maybe of centuries, as the last colonists mined their homes for stuff they could no longer make. We can only be sure, from the dust, that no one's been inside for longer than I like to think about.''

When Regor had signed off, Jong would usually take out his guitar and chord the songs they sang, the immemorial songs of the Kith, many translated from languages spoken before ever men left Earth. It helped drown out the wind and the surf, booming down on the beach where once a harbor had stood. The fire flared high, picking their faces out of night, tinging plain work clothes with unrestful red, and then guttering down so that shadows swallowed the bodies. They looked much alike, those four men, small, lithe, with sharp, dark features; for the Kith were a folk apart, marrying between their own ships, which carried nearly all traffic among the stars. Since a vessel might be gone from Earth for a century or more, the planetbound civilizations, flaring and dying and reborn like the flames that warmed them now, could not be theirs. The men differed chiefly in age, from the sixty years that furrowed Regor Lannis's

skin to the twenty that Jong Errifrans had marked not '
long ago.

Ship's years, mostly, Jong remembered, and
looked up to the Milky Way with a shudder. When
you fled at almost the speed of light, time shrank for
you, and in his own life he had seen the flower and
the fall of an empire. He had not thought much
about it then—it was the way of things, that the
Kith should be quasi-immortal and the planetarians
alien, transitory, not quite real. But a voyage of ten
thousand light-years toward galactic center, and
back, was more than anyone had ventured before;
more than anyone would ever have done, save to
expiate the crime of crimes. Did the Kith still exist?
Did Earth?

After some days, Regor decided: "We'd better
take a look at the hinterland. We may improve our
luck."

"Nothing in the interior but forest and savan-
nah," Neri Avelair objected. "We saw that from
above."

"On foot, though, you see items you miss from a
boat," Regor said. "The colonists can't have lived ex-
clusively in places like this. They'd need farms,
mines, extractor plants, outlying settlements. If we
could examine one of those, we might find clearer
indications than in this damned huge warren."

"How much chance would we have, hacking our
way through the brush?" Neri argued. "I say let's
investigate some of those other towns we spotted."

"They're more ruined yet," Mons Rainart reminded him. "Largely submerged." He need not
have spoken; how could they forget? Land does not

sink fast. The fact that the sea was eating the cities gave some idea of how long they had been abandoned.

"Just so." Regor nodded. "I don't propose plunging into the woods, either. That'd need more men and more time than we can spare. But there's an outsize beach about a hundred kilometers north of here, fronting on a narrow-mouthed bay, with fertile hills right behind—hills that look as if they ought to contain ores. I'd be surprised if the colonists did not exploit the area."

Neri's mouth twitched downward. His voice was not quite steady. "How long do we have to stay on this ghost planet before we admit we'll never know what happened?"

"Not too much longer," Regor said. "But we've got to try our best before we do leave."

He jerked a thumb at the city. Its towers soared above fallen walls and marching dunes into a sky full of birds. The bright yellow sun had bleached out their pastel colors, leaving them bone-white. And yet the view on their far side was beautiful, forest that stretched inland a hundred shades of shadow-rippled green, while in the opposite direction the land sloped down to a sea that glittered like emerald strewn with diamond dust, moving and shouting and hurling itself in foam against the reefs. The first generations here must have been very happy, Jong thought.

"Something destroyed them, and it wasn't simply a war," Regor said. "We need to know what. It may not have affected any other world. But maybe it did."

Maybe Earth lay as empty, Jong thought, not for

the first time.

The *Golden Flyer* had paused here to refit before venturing back into man's old domain. Captain Ilmaray had chosen an F9 star arbitrarily, three hundred light-years from Sol's calculated present position. They detected no whisper of the energies used by civilized races, who might have posed a threat. The third planet seemed a paradise, Earth-mass but with its land scattered in islands around a global ocean, warm from pole to pole. Mons Rainart was surprised that the carbon dioxide equilibrium was maintained with so little exposed rock. Then he observed weed mats everywhere on the waters, many of them hundreds of square kilometers in area, and decided that their photosynthesis was active enough to produce a Terrestrial-type atmosphere.

The shock had been to observe from orbit the ruined cities. Not that colonization could not have reached this far, and beyond, during twenty thousand years. But the venture had been terminated; why?

That evening it was Jong's turn to hold a personal conversation with those in the mother ship. He got his parents, via intercom, to tell them how he fared. The heart jumped in his breast when Sorya Rainart's voice joined theirs. "Oh yes," the girl said, with an uneven little laugh, "I'm right here in the apartment. Dropped in for a visit, by chance."

Her brother chuckled at Jong's back. The young man flushed and wished hotly for privacy. But of course Sorya would have known he'd call tonight . . . . If the Kith still lived, there could be nothing between him and her. You brought your wife home from another ship. It was spaceman's law, exogamy aiding a survival that was precarious at best. If, though, the last Kith ship but theirs drifted dead among the stars; or the few hundred aboard the *Golden Flyer* and the four on this world whose name was lost were the final remnants of the human race— she was bright and gentle and swayed sweetly when she walked.

"I—" He untangled his tongue. "I'm glad you did. How are you?"

"Lonely and frightened," she confided. Cosmic interference seethed around her words. The fire spat sparks loudly into the darkness overhead. "If you don't learn what went wrong here . . . . I don't know if I can stand wondering the rest of my life."

"Cut that!" he said sharply. The rusting of morale had destroyed more than one ship in the past. Although— "No, I'm sorry." He knew she did not lack courage. The fear was alive in him too that he would be haunted forever by what he had seen here. Death in itself was an old familiar of the Kith. But this time they were returning from a past more ancient than the glaciers and the mammoths had been on Earth when they left. They needed knowledge as much as they needed air, to make sense of the universe. And their first stop in that spiral arm of the Galaxy which had once been home had confronted them with a riddle that looked unanswerable. So deep in history were the roots of the Kith that Jong could recall the symbol of the Sphinx; and suddenly he saw how gruesome it was.

"We'll find out," he promised Sorya. "If not here, then when we arrive at Earth." Inwardly he was unsure. He made small talk and even achieved a joke or two. But afterward, laid out in his sleeping bag, he thought he heard the horn winding in the north.

The expedition rose at dawn, bolted breakfast, and stowed their gear in the spaceboat. It purred from the city on aerodynamic drive, leveled off, flew at low speed not far above ground. The sea tumbled and flashed on the right, the land climbed steeply on the left. No herds of large animals could be seen there. Probably none existed, with such scant room to develop in. But the ocean swarmed. From above Jong could look down into transparent waters, see shadows that were schools of fish numbering in the hundreds of thousands. Further off he observed a herd of grazers, piscine but big as whales, plowing slowly through a weed mat. The colonists must have gotten most of their living from the sea.

Regor set the boat down on a cliff overlooking the bay he had described. The escarpment ringed a curved beach of enormous length and breadth, its sands strewn with rocks and boulders. Kilometers away, the arc closed in on itself, leaving only a strait passage to the ocean. The bay was placid, clear bluish-green beneath the early sun, but not stagnant. The tides of the one big moon must raise and lower it two or three meters in a day, and a river ran in from the southern highlands. Afar Jong could see how shells littered the sand below high-water mark, proof of abundant life. It seemed bitterly unfair to him that the colonists had had to trade so much beauty for darkness.

Regor's lean face turned from one man to the next. "Equipment check," he said, and went down the list: fulgurator, communication bracelet, energy compass, medikit—"My God," said Neri, "you'd think we were off on a year's trek, and separately at that."

"We'll disperse, looking for traces," Regor said, "and those rocks will often hide us from each other." He left the rest unspoken: that that which had been the death of the colony might still exist.

They emerged into cool, flowing air with the salt and iodine and clean decay smell of coasts on every Earthlike world, and made their way down the scarp. "Let's radiate from this point," Regor said, "and if nobody has found anything, we'll meet back here in four hours for lunch."

Jong's path slanted farthest north. He walked briskly at first, enjoying the motion of his muscles, the scrunch of sand and rattle of pebbles beneath his boots, the whistle of the many birds overhead. But presently he must pick his way across drifts of stone and among dark boulders, some as big as houses, which cut him off from the wind and his fellows; and he remembered Sorya's aloneness.

Oh no, not that. Haven't we paid enough? he thought. And, for a moment's defiance: *We didn't do the thing. We condemned the traitors ourselves, and threw them into space, as soon as we learned. Why should we be punished?*

But the Kith had been too long isolated, themselves against the universe, not to hold that the sin and sorrow of one belonged to all. And Tomakan and his coconspirators had done what they did unselfishly, to save the ship. In those last vicious years of the Star Empire, when Earthmen made the Kithfolk

scapegoats for their wretchedness until every crew
fled to await better times, the *Golden Flyer*'s captured people would have died horribly—had
Tomakan not bought their freedom by betraying to
the persecutors that asteroid where two other Kith
vessels lay, readying to leave the Solar System. How
could they afterward meet the eyes of their kindred,
in the Council that met at Tau Ceti?

The sentence was just: to go exploring to the
fringes of the galactic nucleus. Perhaps they would
find the Elder Races that must dwell somewhere;
perhaps they could bring back the knowledge and
wisdom that could heal man's inborn lunacies. Well,
they hadn't; but the voyage was something in itself,
sufficient to give the *Golden Flyer* back her honor.
No doubt everyone who had sat in Council was now
dust. Still, their descendants—

Jong stopped in midstride. His shout went ringing
among the rocks.

"What is it? Who called? Anything wrong?" The
questions flew from his bracelet like anxious bees.

He stooped over a little heap and touched it with
fingers that wouldn't hold steady. "Worked flints,"
he breathed. "Flakes, broken spearheads . . .
shaped wood . . . something—" He scrabbled in the
sand. Sunlight struck off a piece of metal, rudely
hammered into a dagger. It had been, it must have
been fashioned from some of the ageless alloy in the
city—long ago, for the blade was worn so thin that it
had snapped across. He crouched over the shards and
babbled.

And shortly Mons' deep tones cut through:
"Here's another site! An animal skull, could only

have been split with a sharp stone, a thong— Wait, wait, I see something carved in this block, maybe a symbol—''

Then suddenly he roared, and made a queer choked gurgle, and his voice came to an end.

Jong leaped erect. The communicator jabbered with calls from Neri and Regor. He ignored them. There was no time for dismay. He tuned his energy compass. Each bracelet emitted a characteristic frequency besides its carrier wave, for location purposes, and— The needle swung about. His free hand unholstered his fulgurator, and he went bounding over the rocks.

As he broke out onto the open stretch of sand the wind hit him full in the face. Momentarily through its shrillness he heard the horn, louder than before, off beyond the cliffs. A part of him remembered fleetingly how one day on a frontier world he had seen a band of huntsmen gallop in pursuit of a wounded animal that wept as it ran, and how the chief had raised a crooked bugle to his lips and blown just such a call.

The note died away. Jong's glance swept the beach. Far down its length he saw several figures emerge from a huddle of boulders. Two of them carried a human shape. He yelled and sprinted to intercept them. The compass dropped from his grasp.

They saw him and paused. When he neared, Jong made out that the form they bore was Mons Rainart's. He swung ghastly limp between his carriers. Blood dripped from his back and over his breast.

Jong's stare went to the six murderers. They were chillingly manlike, half a meter taller than him, magnificently thewed beneath the naked white skin, but altogether hairless, with long webbed feet and fingers, a high dorsal fin, and smaller fins at heels and elbows and on the domed heads. The features were bony, with great sunken eyes and no external ears. A flap of skin drooped from pinched nose to wide mouth. Two carried flint-tipped wooden spears, two had tridents forged from metal—the tines of one were red and wet—and those who bore the body had knives slung at their waists.

"Stop!" Jong shrieked. "Let him go!"

He plowed to a halt not far off, and menaced them with his gun. The biggest uttered a gruff bark and advanced, trident poised. Jong retreated a step. Whatever they had done, he hated to—

An energy beam winked, followed by its thunderclap. The one who carried Mons' shoulders crumpled, first at the knees, then down into the sand. The blood from the hole burned through him mingled with the spaceman's, equally crimson.

They whirled. Neri Avelair pounded down the beach from the opposite side. His fulgurator spoke again. The shimmering wet sand reflected the blast. It missed, but quartz fused where it struck near the feet of the creatures, and hot droplets spattered them.

The leader waved his trident and shouted. They lumbered toward the water. The one who had Mons' ankles did not let go. The body flapped arms and head as it dragged. Neri shot a third time. Jolted by his own speed, he missed anew. Jong's finger remained frozen on the trigger.

The five giants entered the bay. Its floor shelved rapidly. In a minute they were able to dive below the surface. Neri reached Jong's side and fired, bolt after bolt, till a steam cloud rose into the wind. Tears whipped down his cheeks. "Why didn't you kill them, you bastard?" he screamed. "You could have gunned them down where you were!"

"I don't know." Jong stared at his weapon. It felt oddly heavy.

"They drowned Mons!"

"No . . . he was dead already. I could see. Must have been pierced through the heart. I suppose they ambushed him in those rocks—"

"M-m-maybe. But his body, God damn you, we could'a saved that at least!" Senselessly, Neri put a blast through the finned corpse.

"Stop that," commanded Regor. He threw himself down, gasping for breath. Dimly, Jong noticed gray streaks in the leader's hair. It seemed a matter of pity and terror that Regor Lannis the unbendable should be whittled away by the years.

What am I thinking? Mons is killed. Sorya's brother.

Neri holstered his fulgurator, covered his face with both hands, and sobbed.

After a long while Regor shook himself, rose, knelt again to examine the dead swimmer. "So there were natives here," he muttered. "The colonists must not have known. Or maybe they underestimated what savages could do."

His hands ran over the glabrous hide. "Still warm," he said, almost to himself. "Air-breathing; a true mammal, no doubt, though this male lacks vestigial nipples; real nails on the digits, even if they have grown as thick and sharp as claws." He peeled back the lips and examined the teeth. "Omnivore evolving toward carnivore, I'd guess. The molars are still pretty flat, but the rest are bigger than ours, and rather pointed." He peered into the dimmed eyes. "Human-type vision, probably less acute. You can't see so far underwater. We'll need extensive study to determine the color-sensitivity curve, if any. Not to mention the other adaptations. I daresay they can stay below for many minutes at a stretch. Doubtless not as long as cetaceans, however. They haven't evolved that far from their land ancestors. You can tell by the fins. Of some use in swimming, but not really an efficient size or shape as yet."

"You can speculate about that while Mons is being carried away?" Neri choked.

Regor got up and tried in a bemused fashion to brush the sand off his clothes. "Oh no," he said. His face worked, and he blinked several times. "We've got to do something about him, of course." He looked skyward. The air was full of wings, as the sea birds sensed meat and wheeled insolently close. Their piping overrode the wind. "Let's get back to the boat. We'll take this carcass along for the scientists."

Neri cursed at the delay, but took one end of the object. Jong had the other. The weight felt monstrous, and seemed to grow while they stumbled toward the cliffs. Breath rasped in their throats. Their shirts clung to the sweat on them, which they could smell through every sea odor.

Jong looked down at the ugly countenance beneath his hands. In spite of everything, in spite of Mons being dead—oh, never to hear his big laugh again, never to move a chessman or hoist a glass or stand on the thrumming decks with him!—he wondered if a female dwelt somewhere out in the ocean who had thought this face was beautiful.

"We weren't doing them any harm," said Neri between wheezes.

"You can't . . . blame a poison snake . . . or a carnivore . . . if you come too near," Jong said.

"But these aren't dumb animals! Look at that braincase. At that knife." Neri needed a little time before he had the lungful to continue his fury: "We've dealt with nonhumans often enough. Fought them once in a while. But they had a reason to fight . . . mistaken or not, they did. I never saw or heard of anyone striking down utter strangers at first sight."

"We may not have been strangers," Regor said.

"What?" Neri's head twisted around to stare at the older man.

Regor shrugged. "A human colony was planted here. The natives seem to have wiped it out. I imagine they had reasons then. And the tradition may have survived."

For ten thousand years or more? Jong thought, shocked. *What horror did our race visit on theirs, that they haven't been able to forget in so many millennia?*

He tried to picture what might have happened, but found no reality in it, only a dry and somehow thin logic. Presumably this colony was established by a successor civilization to the Star Empire. Presumably that civilization had crumbled in its turn. The settlers had most likely possessed no spaceships of their own; outpost worlds found it easiest to rely on the Kith for what few trade goods they wanted. Often their libraries did not even include the technical data for building a ship, and they lacked the economic surplus necessary to do that research over again.

So—the colony was orphaned. Later, if a period of especially virulent anti-Kithism had occurred here, the traders might have stopped coming; might actually have lost any record of this world's existence. *Or the Kith might have become extinct, but that is not a possibility we will admit.* The planet was left isolated.

Without much land surface it couldn't support a very big population, even if most of the food and industrial resources had been drawn from the sea. However, the people should have been able to maintain a machine culture. No doubt their society would ossify, but static civilizations can last indefinitely.

Unless they are confronted by vigorous barbarians, organized into million-man hordes under the lash of outrage . . . . But was that the answer? Given atomic energy, how could a single city be overrun by any number of neolithic hunters?

Attack from within? A simultaneous revolt of every autochthonous slave? Jong looked back to the dead face. The teeth glinted at him. *Maybe I'm soft-headed. Maybe these beings simply take a weasel's pleasure in killing.*

They struggled up the scarp and into the boat. Jong was relieved to get the thing hidden in a cold-storage locker. But then came the moment when they called the *Golden Flyer* to report.

"I'll tell his family," said Captain Ilmaray, most quietly.

But I'll still have to tell Sorya how he looked, Jong thought. The resolution stiffened in him: *We're going to recover the body. Mons is going to have a Kithman's funeral; hands that loved him will start him on his orbit into the sun.*

He had no reason to voice it, even to himself. The oneness of the Kith reached beyond death. Ilmaray asked only if Regor believed there was a chance.

"Yes, provided we start soon," the leader replied. "The bottom slopes quickly here, but gets no deeper than about thirty meters. Then it's almost flat to some distance beyond the gate, farther than our sonoprobes reached when we flew over. I doubt the swimmers go so fast they can evade us till they reach a depth too great for a nucleoscope to detect Mons' electronic gear."

"Good. Don't take risks, though." Grimly: "We're too short on future heredity as is." After a pause, Ilmaray added, "I'll order a boat with a high-powered magnascreen to the stratosphere, to keep your general area under observation. Luck ride with you."

"And with every ship of ours," Regor finished the formula.

As his fingers moved across the pilot board, raising the vessel, he said over his shoulder, "One of you two get into a spacesuit and be prepared to go down. The other watch the 'scope, and lower him when we find what we're after."

"I'll go," said Jong and Neri into each other's

mouths. They exchanged a look. Neri's glared.

"Please," Jong begged. "Maybe I ought to have shot them down, when I saw what they'd done to Mons. I don't know. But anyhow, I didn't. So let me bring him back, will you?"

Neri regarded him for nearly a minute more before he nodded.

The boat cruised in slow zigzags out across the bay while Jong climbed into his spacesuit. It would serve as well underwater as in the void. He knotted a line about his waist and adjusted the other end to the little winch by the personnel lock. The metallic strand woven into its plastic would conduct phone messages. He draped a sack over one arm for the, well, the search object, and hoped he would not need the slugthrower at his hip.

"There!"

Jong jerked at Neri's shout. Regor brought the craft to hoverhalt, a couple of meters above the surface and three kilometers from shore. "You certain?" he asked.

"Absolutely. Not moving, either. I suppose they abandoned him so as to make a faster escape when they saw us coming through the air."

Jong clamped his helmet shut. External noises ceased. The stillness made him aware of his own breath and pulse and—some inner sound, a stray nerve current or mere imagination—the hunter's horn, remote and triumphant.

The lock opened, filling with sky. Jong walked to the rim and was nearly blinded by the sunlight off the wavelets. Radiance ran to the horizon. He eased himself over the lip. The rope payed out and the surface shut above him. He sank.

A cool green roofed with sunblaze enclosed him. Even through the armor he felt multitudinous vibrations; the sea lived and moved, everywhere around. A pair of fish streaked by, unbelievably graceful. For a heretical instant he wondered if Mons would not rather stay here, lulled to the end of the world.

Cut that! he told himself, and peered downward. Darkness lurked below. He switched on the powerful flash at his belt.

Particles in the water scattered the light, so that he fell as if through an illuminated cave. More fish passed near. Their scales reflected like jewels. He thought he could make out the bottom now, white sand and uplifted ranges of rock on which clustered many-colored coraloids, growing toward the sun. And the swimmer appeared.

He moved slowly to the fringe of light and poised. In his left hand he bore a trident, perhaps the one which had killed Mons. At first he squinted against the dazzle, then looked steadily at the radiant metal man. As Jong continued to descend he followed, propelling himself with easy gestures of feet and free hand, a motion as lovely as a snake's.

Jong gasped and yanked out his slugthrower.

"What's the matter?" Neri's voice rattled in his earplugs.

He gulped. "Nothing," he said, without knowing why. "Lower away."

The swimmer came a little closer. His muscles were tense, mouth open as if to bite; but the deep-set eyes remained unwavering. Jong returned the gaze. They went down together.

He's not afraid of me, Jong thought, *or else he's*

mastered his fear, though he saw on the beach what we can do.

Impact jarred through his soles. "I'm here," he called mechanically. "Give me some slack and—Oh!"

The blood drained from his head as if an ax had split it. He swayed, supported only by the water. Thunders and winds went through him, and the roar of the horn.

"Jong!" Neri called, infinitely distant. "Something's wrong, I know it is, gimme an answer, for the love of Kith!"

The swimmer touched bottom too. He stood across from what had belonged to Mons Rainart, the trident upright in his hand.

Jong lifted the gun. "I can fill you with metal," he heard himself groan. "I can cut you to pieces, the way you—you—"

The swimmer shuddered (was the voice conducted to him?) but stayed where he was. Slowly, he raised the trident toward the unseen sun. With a single gesture, he reversed it, thrust it into the sand, let go, and turned his back. A shove of the great legs sent him arrowing off.

The knowledge exploded in Jong. For a century of seconds he stood alone with it.

Regor's words pierced through: "Get my suit. I'm going after him."

"I'm all right," he managed to say. "I found Mons."

He gathered what he could. There wasn't much. "Bring me up," he said.

When he was lifted from the bay and climbed

through the air lock, he felt how heavy was the weight upon him. He let fall the sack and trident and crouched beside them. Water ran off his armor.

The doors closed. The boat climbed. A kilometer high, Regor locked the controls and came aft to join the others. Jong removed his helmet just as Neri opened the sack.

Mons' head rolled out and bounced dreadfully across the deck. Neri strangled a yell.

Regor lurched back. "They ate him," he croaked. "They cut him to pieces for food. Didn't they?"

He gathered his will, strode to the port, and squinted out. "I saw one of them break the surface, a short while before you came up," he said between his teeth. Sweat—or was it tears?—coursed down the gullies in his cheeks. "We can catch him. The boat has a gun turret."

"No—" Jong tried to rise, but hadn't the strength.

The radio buzzed. Regor ran to the pilot's chair forward, threw himself into it, and slapped the receiver switch. Neri set lips together, picked up the head, and laid it on the sack. "Mons, Mons, but they'll pay," he said.

Captain Ilmaray's tones filled the hull: "We just got word from the observer's boat. It isn't on station yet, but the magnascreen's already spotted a horde of swimmers . . . no, several different flocks, huge, must total thousands . . . converging on the island where you are. At the rate they're going, they should arrive in a couple of days."

Regor shook his head in a stunned fashion. "How did they know?"

"They didn't," Jong mumbled.

Neri leaped to his feet, a tiger movement. "That's exactly the chance we want. A couple of bombs dropped in the middle of 'em."

"You mustn't!" Jong cried. He became able to rise too. The trident was gripped in his hand. "He gave me this."

"What?" Regor swiveled around. Neri stiffened where he stood. Silence poured through the boat.

"Down below," Jong told them. "He saw me and followed me to the bottom. Realized what I was doing. Gave me this. His weapon."

"Whatever *for?*"

"A peace offering. What else?"

Neri spat on the deck. "Peace, with those filthy cannibals?"

Jong squared his shoulders. The armor enclosing him no longer seemed an insupportable burden. "You wouldn't be a cannibal if you ate a monkey, would you?"

Neri said an obscene word, but Regor suppressed him with a gesture. "Well, different species," the pilot admitted coldly. "By the dictionary you're right. But these killers are sentient. You don't eat another thinking being."

"It's been done," Jong said. "By humans too. More often than not as an act of respect or love, taking some of the person's mana into yourself. Anyway, how could they know what we were? When he saw I'd come to gather our dead, he gave me his weapon. How else could he say he was sorry, and that we're brothers? Maybe he even realized that's literally true, after he'd had a little while to think the matter over. But I don't imagine their traditions are that old. It's enough, it's better, actually, that he confessed we were his kin simply because we also care for our dead.''

"What are you getting at?" Neri snapped.

"Yes, what the destruction's going on down there?" Ilmaray demanded through the radio.

"Wait." Regor gripped the arms of his chair. His voice fell low. "You don't mean they're—"

"Yes, I do," Jong said. "What else could they be? How could a mammal that big, with hands and brain, evolve on these few islands? How could any natives have wiped out a colony that had atomic arms? I thought about a slave revolt, but that doesn't make sense either. Who'd bother with so many slaves when they had cybernetic machines? No, the swimmers are the colonists. They can't be anything else.''

"Huh?" grunted Neri.

Ilmaray said across hollow space: "It could be. If I remember rightly, Homo Sapiens is supposed to have developed from the, uh, Neandertaloid type, in something like ten or twenty thousand years. Given a small population, genetic drift, yes, a group might need less time than that to degenerate.''

"Who says they're degenerate?" Jong retorted.

Neri pointed to the staring-eyed head on the deck. "That does.''

"Was an accident, I tell you, a misunderstanding," Jong said. "We had it coming, blundering in blind the way we did. They aren't degenerate, they're just adapted. As the colony got more and more dependent on the sea, and mutations occurred, those who could best take this sort of environment had the most children. A static civilization wouldn't notice what was happening till too late, and wouldn't be able to do anything about it if they did. Because the new people had the freedom of the whole planet. The future was theirs."

"Yeah, a future of being savages."

"They couldn't use our kind of civilization. It's wrong for this world. If you're going to spend most of your life in salt water you can't very well keep your electric machines; and flint you can gather almost anywhere is an improvement over metal that has to be mined and smelted.

"Oh, maybe they have lost some intelligence. I doubt that, but if they have, what of it? We never did find the Elder Races. Maybe intelligence really isn't the goal of the universe. I believe, myself, these people are coming back up the ladder in their own way. But that's none of our business." Jong knelt and closed Mons' eyes. "We were allowed to atone for our crime," he said softly. "The least we can do is forgive them in our turn. Isn't it? And . . . we don't know if any other humans are left, anywhere in all the worlds, except us and these. No, we can't kill them."

"Then why did they kill Mons?"

"They're air breathers," Jong said, "and doubtless they have to learn swimming, like pinnipeds, instead of having an instinct. So they need breeding grounds. That beach, yes, that must be where the tribes are headed. A party of males went in advance to make sure the place was in order. They saw something strange and terrible walking on the ground where their children were to be born, and they had the courage to attack it. I'm sorry, Mons,'' he finished in a whisper.

Neri slumped down on a bench. The silence came back.

Until Ilmaray said: ''I think you have the answer. We can't stay here. Return immediately, and we'll get under weigh.''

Regor nodded and touched the controls. The engine hummed into life. Jong got up, walked to a port, and watched the sea, molten silver beneath him, dwindle as the sky hardened and the stars trod forth.

I wonder what that sound was, he thought vaguely. *A wind noise, no doubt, as Mons said. But I'll never be sure.* For a moment it seemed to him that he heard it again, in the thrum of energy and metal, in the beat of his own blood, the horn of a hunter pursuing a quarry that wept as it ran.